The Orion Nebula Adventure

William Hughes

1-7-11

The Orion Nebula Adventure

William J. Hughes

Tate Publishing & *Enterprises*

Published by Tate Publishing & Enterprises, LLC
127 E. Trade Center Terrace | Mustang, Oklahoma 73064 USA
1.888.361.9473 | www.tatepublishing.com

Tate Publishing is committed to excellence in the publishing industry. The company reflects the philosophy established by the founders, based on Psalm 68:11,
"The Lord gave the word and great was the company of those who published it."

Cover design by Chris Webb
Interior design by Nathan Harmony

Published in the United States of America

ISBN: 978-1-61739-149-1
1. Fiction: Science Fiction: Military
2. Fiction: Science Fiction: Adventure
10.10.01

Dedication

Part 1, "Adventure in the Nebula," is dedicated to Katie and Jennifer. Both have touched my heart in so many ways and have been dear friends since I met them. Katie was only ten hours old when I first met her, and Jennifer was about three and a half.

Part 2, "Panthers Return," is to my twin brother, Walter. I hurriedly wrote this part Easter weekend of 2007 in an attempt to get it to him for our fortieth birthday, but it got there a bit late. His son, Lee, and daughter, Sarah, made their first appearance in this part.

I would also like to make a special dedication to Bethany. She made her first appearance in this part also, upon the request from Jennifer.

Part 3, "Rebellion: At War Once More," is dedicated to Ben and Dylan, because their friendship as youngsters was what I patterned their friendship in the story after.

I also would like to make a special dedication to those young people who were supporting characters upon requests from Katie and Jennifer; they truly made the story better.

Part 4, "Reasons to Continue the Fight," is dedicated to Doris and Deborah because they showed great patience and helped me while writing this story.

Acknowledgments

I would like to acknowledge and thank three people, without whose support and help this story may have never gotten this far: Doris Browning, Deborah Halcomb-Hodge, and Dr. Bruce Ayers.

I would also like to thank anyone who helped me since 2006 by simply encouraging me or giving me feedback about my story. I did not realize it at the time, but it all made my story what it is.

Note to Readers

I had a similar idea for a story like this a long time ago for an assignment in my Junior year English class in high school. I had wanted that story take place in a nebula aboard a space station, with a small group fighting robots. The story back then took a different direction.

Also I had wanted to write a story with my young, dear friend Katie Graham as a major character for a couple of years. The opportunity presented itself in May, 2006, while watching a program about the awesome Apache helicopter on the Military Channel. I got the idea for the spacecraft I named *Vixen*.

While thinking of how the ship might look, I saw in my mind's eye a young woman at the controls piloting the craft into the atmosphere of an alien world. I realized the young woman was Katie, and the idea for the story was born. The other three parts came about because I wanted to continue the story.

My friend, Bruce, once told me that once you write something it takes on a life of its own. This story truly did and matured into the story within these pages.

I chose to use people in our lives as main and supporting characters and created a few fictional ones to give it a true space adventure feel.

I hope you enjoy reading it, as I did writing it.

Part 1

Adventure in the Nebula

The Arrival

The Interstellar Alliance's science station, called *Big Rock,* floats silently in space, near the awesome and beautiful Orion Nebula. The distant and remote sector of space has been home to the small asteroid station for a little over a week. *Big Rock* is accompanied by the large space barge, called *Big Willie*. Since the station's drive engines were yet to be activated, her captain felt it wise to stick around. On the station's command deck things were quiet as the small night crew and service robots went about their tasks. It was late evening, and the petite figure standing at the main viewport seemed out of place.

Katie, the station's commander, stood quietly looking out into space for hours. The day had been long, and exhaustion weighed on her; still, she could not sleep. A special guest was due to arrive at any moment. A short time later, a flash in the star-filled sky caught her attention. She jumped with excitement on the deck, startling the officer closest to her. "Sorry."

She blushed and turned back to the viewport. Whispering to herself, she said, "She's here!"

The flash had been a small fleet exiting light speed, led by her sister's ship, *Tiger's Pride*. The refurbished battle cruiser had escorted the smaller freighters on their supply run to the station.

Jennifer, *the owner* and captain of the Tiger's Pride, walked confidently onto the bridge with her tiger companion, Max, following close behind. A deck officer approached to make a report. The young officer proceeded nervously when he saw the massive Bengal tiger standing at Jennifer's side. "Captain, we have entered the Orion sector."

She acknowledged his report with a nod as she looked out the viewport. "We are here Max."

The tiger growled a response. Although it did not hurt to use the cybernetic headgear, he still felt uncomfortable doing so. She still understood him fine.

This was Max's first spaceflight since getting the cybernetic device surgically attached to his head. Jennifer and Katie's brother Ben, who was a biologist/cybernetic engineer, made Jennifer a proposition a few months earlier. One she jumped at. He had invented a cybernetic device for animals, which was designed to allow verbal communication between humans and animals. He asked if he could fit her tiger companion with it. The cybernetic device made it possible for him to travel with her more often. She hated leaving him at home on Mars because the instability that existed on the colony bothered her. Max became her bodyguard as well as a traveling companion. The two were inseparable; however, the crew was a little nervous having a tiger wandering the ship.

As *Tiger's Pride* and the small freighter fleet approached the station, the two companions admired the view of the nebula, in the distance.

Katie was excited and paced the deck near the airlock door. She thought to herself, *Girl, pull yourself together. You are the commander of this rock*. She could not help it, for she had not seen her big sister in nearly a year.

With a loud clang, the ship had docked. The door opened, and Max leaped through and was the first to reach Katie, knocking her down. She gave him a big hug and looked up at her sister, and she noticed that Jennifer had begun to favor their mother.

"Hi Jennifer, how you been?"

Jennifer replied, "Hi there. I am fine. It is good to see you; it has been a long time. You are looking good." Katie was petite like their grandmother, Oma, and Jennifer was not surprised that her little sister was looking more like their grandmother the older she got. The sisters embraced for several minutes.

After exchanging greetings, the trio turned and entered the elevator for the ride down to the station. Katie broke the silence. "Where did you get that ship?"

Jennifer answered her little sister with a smile on her face. "I got it from Uncle William's company. I bought it at a company auction, and the crew is on loan until Mech 1 and I get the robots online. Willie really helped me out because I can't afford a human crew." Katie thought of her friend. She remembered the first time she called him Willie, and even though he was a family friend she and her siblings always called him Uncle William or Willie.

Katie laughed. "Yeah, he's the best." Katie's thought switched instantly to her father. "Hey, is dad still with Falcon Intergalactic?"

"Yeah, he is still in charge of the company's security division. Oh, he says hi and wishes he could have come along. He sent you something from home. I forgot it back on the ship. We can get it later."

A few moments later in Katie's quarters, Jennifer commented, "Looks the same as when Dad had this place."

Katie agreed with her big sister. "Yeah, it hasn't changed much. The structure is still sound. We just upgraded the main systems, and Boots helped me designed a drive system, and we are in the process of installing it now."

Wide-eyed Jennifer asked curiously, "This rock can travel through space by itself?"

Katie smiled. "Is that cool or what?"

The young women laughed. The sisters talked until they fell asleep, sometime late in the night.

Adventure Bound

Mornings on the moon Phobos' small spaceport were usually peaceful, but not this morning. On this day, an adventurous trio would set out on a long-awaited journey.

The morning silence was shattered by a loud boom and shouting.

Boom! The mechanical load lifter hit the side of the ship.

"Whoa! Tyton, watch what you're doing!" Dylan screamed at his robot partner.

The large robot looked out of the large machine. "Sorry about that sir."

The impact the load lifter made against the ship shook Ben out of his bunk. He stood and stumbled, half asleep, toward the loading ramp and the noise beyond. Ben had to yell to be heard over the sounds the load lifter made as it moved across the deck. His friends turned to look at him and Dylan began laughing. Tyton climbed from the machine and walked over by his friend. "Good morning, sleepyhead. We're getting an early start on loading the ship. We can't wait to get out of here."

"Get dressed and give us a hand out here." Ben looked down and noticed he was still in his shorts.

He laughed. "Well, okay, since I am up."

He turned and went back up the ramp, whispering to himself. "Marines, I just can't figure those two out."

Despite the early start, the morning slipped away into afternoon on the spaceport. The trio sat beside their ship, *Saber II*. Looking up at the ship, Ben asked, "Thought you guys wouldn't be here till tomorrow?"

Dylan replied, pulling papers from his flight suit pocket, "My release orders came up early, and we got off Mars as soon as we could."

Tyton nodded in agreement and went back to work. The other two finished their drinks and caught up on things.

Several more hours passed as final preparations, repairs, and loading went on. It was early evening. Ben finished his business with the spaceport's deck officer and walked across the deck to meet his friends waiting beside the *Saber II*'s rear loading ramp. "Are you eager to takeoff?"

Dylan grinned at him and patted his shoulder as he walked up the ramp. "Ready!"

Ben followed him. The ship's small maintenance robot rolled in just before it closed behind them. It whistled as it moved toward its storage clamps.

Ben turned and looked at it. "Hi there, little guy. We almost left you."

The little robot whistled in agreement. They laughed as they headed for the cockpit.

The engines rumbled to life with the familiar sound of a ship preparing to take off. Dylan received clearance to lift off, and the *Saber II* left the safety of the hangar into the Mars-filled sky. Dylan looked to his friend. "Where do we go first?"

"The Orion Nebula is a good place to start. I would like to see my sisters. Katie is stationed there aboard *Big Rock* science station. She said Jennifer would be there too. She is escorting a supply fleet in her new ship *Tiger's Pride*. I can check Max's translation device while we are there."

Dylan and Tyton piloted the ship around Mars's horizon. The trio looked at Mars one last time silently. After a moment Tyton broke the silence. "Coordinates are set. Whenever you are ready, sir, we can make the jump."

The friends looked out toward the stars. "Let's go, guys."

Dylan hit a switch and pushed the throttle forward, and with a jerk, the ship jumped into light speed and into adventure.

The Gang Is All Here

Jennifer awoke with a painful jerk and her neck was throbbing because of the position she had been lying in. The chair she slept in was a comfortable one to sit in but not for sleeping. Looking around the room with sleep still in her eyes, she noticed that Katie was not there. Seeing what time it was, she figured she had gone to work. Max was sleeping next to her, and by the noises he made, she could tell it was not a comfortable slumber.

She shook her tiger friend to wake him and said, "Max, are you okay?" The tiger jumped up, growling.

"Hey!" Jennifer smiled. "You've never been easy to get up and always been grouchy in the morning." He glared at her.

"This thing Ben put on my head bothered me all night."

"Max, Ben said it would take time to adjust to it. I will have him look at it the next time we see him."

Growling in pain, he replied, "This is different. The pain started after we got here." Jennifer got up, and she noticed the chair she had slept in. She remembered playing in the same chair while her dad worked at his desk. She rubbed Max's head as she headed for the bathroom.

"We will call Ben and ask him what he thinks. Okay?"

Max growled a response and lay back down for a few more minutes of sleep.

Later on, Jennifer and Max found Katie on the command deck. As they approached her, they could see she was busy, so they held back a moment and looked around. Jennifer noticed the numerous control panels and machinery. She also noticed how the crew performed their tasks with professionalism and efficiency. Jennifer thought to herself, *Impressive setup here. It sure has changed in here since dad had this station.*

A voice sounded from Katie's console. It was the captain of *Big Willie*. "Okay, Commander, give us a call if you need anything. We will be in the sector setting communication beacons a while longer."

Leaning forward she replied, "Roger, Captain. We will do. We should be okay now that our drive engines are up and running."

Katie looked out the viewport as the large barge moved away.

Jennifer walked up behind her and said, "*Big Willie.* I love that name. Kind of fits, doesn't it?"

Katie looked up with a smile on her face. "Yeah it sure does."

Katie turned in her chair as she pushed away from her command console. She scratched behind Max's ear before standing. He rumbled and moved his head in response. "Yeah, big guy, you always liked that."

She stood and reached for a big cup of coffee, "Morning, sis. Want a cup? I have a feeling this cup will be my companion today."

Jennifer answered with a big yawn. "No, I am okay. I had two cups already."

The two women laughed. Both were tired from the long night before.

An officer approached them from across the command deck. Jennifer noticed he had a mechanical arm and cybernetic translation devices over his ears. She thought to herself, *Cyborg translator*.

Katie turned to him, sipping her coffee, and lowered her cup as she spoke. "Yes?"

"Here are the manifests from last night's shipment."

"Thanks."

Katie turned back to Jennifer. "Jen, this is Boots, my translator officer and second in command here. He is boss when I am gone."

Boots smiled shyly and extended his hand. "Nice meeting you. I've heard a lot about you."

Jennifer replied with her always-friendly smile. "Good to meet you."

Katie looked back at her big sister, disappointed. "Sorry, sis, it has been a busy morning. Can I meet you guys later for a late breakfast?"

"That's cool. I need to go up to *Tiger's Pride* and get some things."

Katie and Boots turned to leave, but Max nudged her hand. He did not want to be left out. "Oh! Sorry. Boots, this is our friend Max."

The officer took a short step back cautiously. "Good to meet you!"

Jennifer pulled Max's tail. "Come on, you big fur ball. Let's go up to the ship."

He turned to follow her, shaking his tail, as if she had hurt it. She looked at Boots and smiled.

"Max, I just love when people meet you!" He growled in agreement.

Later at breakfast, the sisters caught up a little more. The meal was cut short by a call from the command deck. "Commander, you have a call coming in."

"I'll take it here."

The static on the speaker was replaced by a familiar voice. "Hi, Katie." The two women screamed.

"Ben!" Katie said into the microphone excitedly. "What arc you doing way out here?"

Ben answered in his usual brotherly way, "Well, we wanted to start our adventures and decided here would be a good place to start."

Behind Ben, voices could be heard. "Ready to exit light speed, sir."

"On my mark, Tyton," Ben said over the sounds of his friends piloting the ship. "We will be there soon."

Dylan's voice replaced Ben's. "This is the *Saber II* requesting permission to come aboard, Commander."

She replied excitedly, "Granted, *Saber II.* You can land in docking bay two. Follow the landing beacons."

Jennifer and Katie looked out the window just in time to see Dylan's famous macho flyby. Laughing, the women turned and ran for the docking bay.

"The gang is all here!" Katie said as they ran.

Tension Fills the Air (Max Goes Down)

The two young women arrived in the docking bay just as the deck control robot was directing the *Saber II* where to set down. Her landing thrusters fired, and she rested on the deck with a loud thump.

They walked over to the ship and waited excitedly as the loading ramp lowered. Dylan was the first to walk down, followed by Tyton. With a smile, he said, "Well! Hi there, ladies. Ben is grabbing his bag."

They both spoke at the same time. "Hi there, Dylan how are you."

The sounds of footsteps at the top the ramp caught Katie's attention, and she looked up for her brother. "Ben!"

He walked down the ramp stretching his back. The siblings hugged as a group. Dylan and Tyton turned to the ship. "We'll give you guys a minute. I need to do a post-flight check on my baby." The trio exchanged greetings a short while longer.

Ben noticed someone was missing and spoke up, "Hey, Jen, where is Max?" She looked around puzzled.

"He was behind us a few minutes ago."

They began a search for their friend. Katie spoke into her headset communication unit. "Command, locate Max."

A static voice answered, "He is in hallway four, Commander, and he is unconscious!"

Katie looked at her sister horrified. "Jen, he is in hallway four. He is unconscious!" Jennifer sprinted for the door, followed closely by Katie. Katie spoke into her headset as she ran.

"Command, I want a medical unit there now!"

Ben looked back at his friends before following his sisters. Dylan nodded to him with a worried look. "Go! We can get this." Ben turned and ran after his sisters.

Later on at the medical center, the small group stood waiting for news about their tiger friend. Jennifer wiped the tears from her face as she watched from behind the glass, thinking to herself how the majestic tiger seemed lifeless on the medical table. Her brother turned, smiled, and then spoke in her direction. She could not hear him, but read his lips. "He is fine."

She smiled.

Boots joined the group as Ben exited the examination room. He looked at Ben. "You need me, sir?"

Ben replied, "Yes, Boots, I need your assistance. I'll explain." He turned to his sisters. "He will be okay. It is his cybernetic translation unit."

Jennifer screamed at him, "You said it was safe!"

Grabbing her shoulders to calm and reassure her, he said, "It is. Just needs to be adjusted." He spoke to the group, "Hey, guys, can you give me awhile? I'll explain soon."

Jennifer and Katie protested; but he reassured them, and they agreed to leave. Holding hands, the sisters headed for the door. Dylan tried to cheer them up as he and Tyton followed them. "Ben is good at what he does. Max will be okay. You'll see."

Jennifer looked back at her tiger friend once more, worried. Ben and Boots started for the examination room. Ben asked, "Are things always this tense here?"

Boots laughed. "Yes, sir, tension seems to come with the job on this rock."

An Amazing Discovery

Jennifer got a bad headache from worrying about Max so she took a nap to try to relieve it. After the call from Ben Katie shook her sister to wake her, and Jennifer jumped up, looking around and calling out for her friend. "Hey, Max!"

Katie comforted her sister. "He is with Ben, and he is okay."

Leaping to her feet and running for the door, she asked, "Where are they?"

Katie replied, "In the science lab, and Ben just called for us to join them."

Jennifer was out the door before her sister could finish.

The door opened, revealing a blushing Jennifer. "Where did you say they were again?"

Laughing, Katie said, "The science lab. Come on. I'll show you."

A few moments later, they found Dylan outside the lab door, and he looked puzzled. He spoke first. "You two know what's going on?" They shook their heads.

"No, but Ben said we would be surprised."

Turning toward the door, Dylan said, "He called me saying I should meet him here. He said something about him finding our first adventure." Katie keyed the door, and the trio stepped inside.

Max ran to meet them, almost knocking them down, and Jennifer hugged him tightly. "Don't scare me like that again, you big fur ball!"

The group walked over to where Ben was sitting. He was grinning from ear to ear. Boots sat working at a console close by. He had not even noticed the others enter, because he could not hear without his cybernetic implant operating. Katie spoke. "Ben, what's going on? You mind explaining it to us?"

"Okay, hold on. Give me a second."

He looked at Boots and put his hand on his shoulder. The cyborg picked up the communication device he had been working on and replaced it into his headgear. Turning, he acknowledged the others.

"Well, hello." He looked to Ben. "I got it, Ben. We will need to go to communications."

Ben looked at the others. "I'll explain on the way."

Dylan shouted toward his friend, "What's going on, man?"

Shhhh!

He turned in the direction of the sound and saw that Max had made the sound.

"Wow," he whispered. He had not heard the big cat using his translation device yet. "Ben is good at what he does!"

The group walked down the hall. No one talked. They listened closely to Ben. His excitement showed in his voice. "You see Max's translation device wasn't malfunctioning, just the opposite. It has been working perfectly. It received signals it is not designed to translate. This caused him to experience extreme pain. We think the last signal caused him to blackout due to an overload."

"What kind of signals, and where are they coming from?" Katie asked.

He answered her a little uncertain. "We are not sure. All we got is a frequency to go on."

The group arrived at the command deck still confused but very curious. Boots got busy at the communications console right away. Jennifer scratched Max on the head as she asked Ben, "Will this device bother him again?"

Ben looked at her reassuringly. "No. I adjusted it, and it is working great now."

Jennifer felt more relieved upon hearing that Max's translation device would not hurt him anymore.

Dylan became anxious and asked once more. "Are you going to tell more?" Ben began to explain. "We are looking for the frequency we found. I adjusted Boots' translation gear to pick up the signal from the communications array."

They walked over to watch Boots. He turned as they approached him. He picked up a connection cable and attached it to his headgear and then put the other end in the console. "Ready."

Ben leaned over to get a better look. "Are you getting anything?"

The cyborg officer looked at him. "No, I don't have anything yet. I'll keep trying."

A couple hours passed without anything happening. Katie fell asleep in her chair. Jennifer told Ben, "Let her sleep. We were up late last night. We can wake her if we get something."

Max walked over and lay at her feet. He wanted to make sure his youngest friend would not be disturbed.

Dylan walked over. "I'm going to get a drink. Want anything?"

Stretching, Ben said, "Yeah."

Dylan returned shortly with something for everyone. Tyton had joined him.

They found a seat. He called over to Boots, "Try searching in the sensor logs. The array aboard the *Saber II* receives stuff all the time and stores it."

Ben agreed.

Boots looked up and smiled and returned his attention to the console. Talking to himself, he said, "That might work." He called his aide to assist him. TU-413 rolled over to assist him.

Most of the group had fallen asleep late in the evening, including Boots. He was slumped over his station beside Katie, as she looked at the glowing monitor. She had awoken from her power nap ready to help and let the others sleep and worked quietly with TU-413. A beep from the console got her attention.

"I got a signal match, Commander. It was recorded shortly after our arrival outside the nebula," the robot said in his static voice.

She replied, "Confirm it."

She shook Boots. "Sleepy head, help him."

He jerked. His eyes opened wide. "Oh my God, we got something."

Katie woke the others, and they gathered around Boots's station. "Can you translate it?"

He answered confidently, "Yes, I think so."

TU-413 began the translation. When he finished, he said, "Translation complete."

Boots hit the printer button and the translation began. When it finished, the group looked down at the page. Printed in red they read the words "*Humans too close.*" The group shared a feeling of shock. Ben looked at all of them and picked up the piece of paper.

"What an amazing discovery!"

Into the Nebula

The excited group gathered in the command center's briefing room after a few hours of sleep. All had agreed a break was needed, and it would be wise to get a fresh start.

Dylan and Boots leaned against the rail at the front of the room. The two had arrived early and were getting acquainted. Dylan noticed the name on Boots' uniform was not the same as what the others had been calling him. He was curious. "Why do the others call you Boots?"

The cyborg officer replied by placing a foot on a nearby chair.

Dylan looked down. "Wow! Are those cowboy boots?"

Boots smiled proudly. "Oh yeah, I know a Texan back on Earth who still makes them as a hobby. I had them fitted for comfort. I just love them, and that's how I got my nickname, Boots."

Boots' aide approached the pair. They looked at the robot. "Are you ready, TU-413?"

"Yes, sir I have completed my preparations." The robot walked across the room.

Dylan look puzzled at the robot and thought aloud. "Wasn't he taller and rolling around here last night?" Just as he finished his thought, the busy robot reached into an empty mobility pod for his data pad.

"Oh! I should get Tyton one of those."

Boots laughed.

Tyton entered the room, found a seat, and waved a greeting to his friend. The others arrived a short time later. They were eager to get started. Boots looked at them and spoke, "Morning, guys. My aide, TU-413, processed the data last night, and we are ready to get started."

Katie found her seat and said, "Cool; let's get to it then."

The door opened. They all turned. The tiger, Max, crawled in low, trying not to be noticed by his friends.

Jennifer could not resist. "Morning, Max. Sleep late, did you?"

Laughing, Ben prompted Boots to continue.

"After our discovery last night, I instructed TU-413 to create a listing of signal matches and categorize by importance. The list is long."

He turned to TU-413, who switched on the hologram projector. An image of the nearby Orion Nebula filled the front portion of the room. Pointing at the image, he explained, "We also determined the origin of the signal came from right here." A green circle briefly appeared on the display and was replaced by the image of strange planet. The group sighed.

Boots continued, "Yes, a planet! We found it using the telescopes after we calculated the direction the signals were coming from."

Dylan whispered to his robot friend sitting next to him, "Standard procedure when possible."

An image of the station appeared inside a yellow circle. Jennifer spoke up, "Is that what I think it is?"

Ben answered, "An immediate threat zone. All space stations and ships have one for security reasons."

Boots agreed, "Yes it is our stations. The signal that caused Max's blackout was within this zone. It came up on the computer sometime early this morning and TU-413 notified me. We got on it immediately."

Max moved closer, more interested now. "Signals of this type are carried on a tight beam, but a solar flare from the nearest star caused it to scatter. We would not have noticed it if Max had not been here."

Katie stood up and moved to the front. "What did it say?"

Boots flipped a switch. A static-filled translated message filled the room. "*More humans arrived.*" The group became unsettled once again.

Dylan stood and shouted above the others, "I think we need to go there and investigate."

The others knew where he was referring to and looked toward the small image of the planet. Boots turned to his commanding officer. "He is correct. I feel it would be dangerous, but necessary to investigate. With your permission, I would like to start planning a mission to the planet."

Katie reluctantly agreed. "Okay. Keep in mind we all go or no one goes."

The others gathered at the front of the room to begin planning the mission.

Several hours passed, every minute filled with some kind of planning and preparation for the upcoming mission.

Katie entered docking bay one and waved to the small group waiting there. Ben joined her, and they walked over to the others. Dylan asked, puzzled. "Why are we in here? The *Saber II* is next door."

Katie did not want to hurt her friend's feelings. "We won't be taking her." With disappointment on his face, Dylan looked in the direction Katie had motioned him to. The sounds of the maintenance deck lift filled the bay. They stood watching as a small craft emerged from below. Dylan's disappointment was replaced by envy and amazement. He was seeing for the first time the ship called *Vixen*.

He leaned towards her and whispered, "Impressive ride."

Katie asked, smiling, "Want to help pilot her?"

Dylan tried unsuccessfully to sound unimpressed. "Okay, if you need me too."

Ben looked up from a container, shaking his head at his friend.

Max was complaining to Jennifer because he wouldn't be going to the planet with them. She explained to him, "We don't have a suit that fits you. I promise I'll get one made for you soon."

Max knew she was right and gave up the argument.

Ben handed out suits to each of them. He explained, "These suits are designed to protect us from alien environments. They will adjust automatically to fit our bodies snugly. Our life signs and scents will be undetectable by the planet's inhabitants."

Katie noticed the letters S.E.P.A. on her suit and asked Ben what they meant. Ben answered her question proudly. "Well, little sis, the letters stand for Self-contained Environmental Protection and Anti-detection, S.E.P.A. for short."

She smiled at him, satisfied with his answer.

The group suited up and boarded the small craft. They all said farewell to their friend who would be left behind. *Vixen*'s engines roared and the small ship lifted off the deck and exited the bay into space. Max looked out the docking bay door as the small ship moved away. TU-413 joined the sad tiger.

Aboard *Vixen*, Katie piloted her ship into the Orion Nebula toward the mystery it held.

The Landing

Tiger's Pride moved away from the *Big Rock Science Station* and drifted in space nearby, like a tiger ready to pounce. The large ship took up a position ready to enter the nebula if needed. Everyone on board knew if the call came, timing would be important.

Max entered the bridge accompanied by TU-413. He could feel the tension, as the officer in command turned and looked at them. His new robot friend rolled over to a communication station to monitor the emergency frequency. He did not join him. He instead went to his favorite spot, beside the captain's chair. The chair was empty for the first time since he had been onboard. His friend had left only a short time ago on a mission into the nebula. He hated being left behind. The sad tiger lay down to wait for his friend's return.

A short time later, Katie's voice sounded from the speaker in the chair beside him. "We have visual of the planet and have taken a position on a nearby asteroid and deployed the sensor pod." Max raised his head. He knew his friends were close to the point of no return, and he felt helpless but knew they could handle themselves.

The small group sat onboard *Vixen* waiting for the sensor pod to complete its survey of the planet below. Several hours passed. The data scrolled across the monitor: 60 percent land surface, 40 percent water, dense forest vegetation, no major surface structures, and 5 energy sources below the surface. Jennifer pushed the record button as she turned from the console.

"What do you think guys?" Her companions seemed optimistic about their mission.

Ben spoke, "The signals definitely came from there. I, for one, sure want to take a closer look."

Dylan and Tyton quickly agreed. "The thick forest will make getting a closer look a bit easier."

Boots spoke up, sounding nervous. "Let's get this over and get back to the station."

Katie smiled at her cyborg partner and began preparations to land. "Here we go!"

She hit a button calling back the sensor pod. A few short moments later, the small craft started its descent into the atmosphere and Jennifer deployed a small communications sphere about the size of a basketball. It was designed to transmit signals using a tight laser beam and would allow the group to communicate with the station without being detected. The group got their gear ready. Dylan watched as Katie piloted her ship toward the planet and could not help being impressed. He wanted to wait till they arrived at their destination to join the others.

An alarm sounded, and Katie deployed the ship's rotor blades, making the descent into the atmosphere less noticeable by those on the planet. *Vixen* flew silently into the cool darkness. After a brief flight, they reached their destination and hovered just above the alien trees. The group, who had named themselves Recon 1 rappelled to the ground. Jennifer leaned out, waving to her brother below as she shut the door and returned to join her little sister. The two women flew to a designated location to wait for a signal from the others

Ben watched as the small ship flew out of sight. He looked back at the others smiling from ear to ear. "Guys, this is so cool."

His friend smiled back at him. "Yeah, we found an adventure, didn't we?"

Tyton interrupted, "Sir, we need to get moving. The sun will be up soon, and according to calculations, we have four to five hours—no more than that." The small group headed east toward the closest power source readings.

Dylan kidded the nervous Boots. "Boots, where are those fancy boots of yours?"

Boots looked at him. "It is time for work, and I think they wouldn't be comfortable here."

He smiled.

Katie set *Vixen* down in a remote area, near a mountain range. Katie retracted the rotor blades and extended the communication pylon. She sighed and looked at her sister. "The rotors will be too slow. I want to be able to get out of here quick."

Jennifer nervously agreed, "I know what you mean."

"Well, we better check in." Jennifer turned to the console and began speaking. "This is Jennifer aboard *Vixen*. We have landed on the planet, and a recon unit is on the ground. Repeat, we have landed."

The signal was received on the bridge of *Tiger's Pride*. "We have landed." Max walked over to the viewport and looked out towards the nebula. Somewhere out there his friends had landed on a strange new world.

A Narrow Escape

Although they had not joined the guys on the ground, the two young women would still play a major part in the mission. Katie and Jennifer could hear everything the group on the ground was saying. Communication was important if the mission was to be successful.

"Recon 1 to ship, come in."

Jennifer answered her brother, "Go ahead, Recon 1. We hear you."

"We have reached the target and are sending in the crawlers for a closer look."

"I copy that Recon 1. We will pick you up when you are ready."

Ben could not hide his excitement. "Jen, this is great. We have discovered an alien race."

Jennifer smiled because she was happy for her brother. All the years of work had finally paid off for him.

Katie yelled up from the rear cabin to her sister. Jennifer put her headset communication unit on and climbed down to see what Katie wanted. She found her little sister standing by a small, tracked vehicle. "Wow! I didn't know you had that."

Katie proudly explained, "It was Mom's, and nobody wanted it, so I kept it. I brought it with me when I got this job and fixed her up."

Jennifer walked over for a closer look. She read the words "Little Maggie" just above the side window. Jennifer turned to her sister with a single tear on her cheek, and Katie began to tear up as well. "I named it in honor of Mom. I thought you might like it." The two remembered too well the events that began the war on Mars. Their mother had been killed in a terrorist attack and Interstellar Alliance Intelligence agents reported she had been the target because she was Earth's ambassador to Mars.

They were brought back to the present by the crackling in their headsets. "Ben, we are getting a signal from our crawler."

Ben answered his friend, "Copy that, Dylan. Send data back to *Vixen*."

Jennifer went to the front of the cabin and sat down at the console. She began to record the incoming data. At that same moment, data started coming in from Ben and

Boots' crawler as well. She adjusted the frequencies and called to the group, "Getting your signals."

She turned back to see what Katie was up to. She was busy removing the straps from the tracked vehicle. "I have an idea. As I see it, we will not be able to pick up the group in *Vixen*." Jennifer listened closely. "We can send Little Maggie to where we dropped them off. They will be able to get back here faster with a little firepower to boot." Katie pointed to the laser cannon turret mounted on top.

Jennifer punched Katie playfully. "You surprise me again, little sis."

Blushing, Katie said, "I had a good teacher."

They both said, "Dad!"

A few moments later, they watched as the small vehicle disappeared into the underbrush. As they turned to go back inside, Katie spoke into her headset communications unit, "Boots, do you copy?" Boots answered, "Go ahead, Commander."

"Boots, I am sending you a little help out there. Proceed to the drop site when you are ready to leave. She will be there."

Smiling toward Ben, Boots answered, "Roger, Commander; will do. Thanks."

Ben looked puzzled, but before Boots could speak, Dylan's voice crackled over the headset communications units. "What kind of help?"

Boots looked in the direction of the drop site. "The commander has a plan." He did not say anything more. Ben was puzzled but did not push it.

He thought to himself, *You'll find out soon enough.*

Back on *Tiger's Pride*, Max listened to every word that came over the speakers and wished he could be there by his friend's side but felt better knowing he was able to hear what they were saying.

Dylan and Tyton returned from the far side of a nearby hill. Tyton carried in his arms one of the small crawlers. He joined Boots, who was just placing his own crawler in a backpack. They joined the others. As they approached, Dylan was telling Ben about what they had seen. "We saw a ship landing over there. It was a fighter as best I could tell, and it seemed familiar too."

Tyton spoke, "An impressive one too, sir."

Ben looked to the horizon and down at the mission chronogram. "Let's get back to the landing site. The sun will be up soon, and we need get out of here fast."

None of the others disagreed. They all ran west into the woods. Boots hesitated a moment and looked back. Shaking his head, he ran after his friends.

A short run later, the group reached the landing site and found, waiting there, Katie's pride and joy. Ben recognized the little vehicle on site. He thought to himself, *It is Mom's old transport. I thought I never would see it again.*

Dylan climbed up and looked down at his friend. "It's got your mom's name on it."

Ben thought aloud. "That was a real nice touch."

Tyton turned to Boots and asked, "Why did you stop back there?"

Boots replied, "I think they know we are here or suspect we are." The large robot leaped on top of the vehicle and climbed into the turret. "We need to depart immediately."

The others climbed in quickly. A note on the control stick read, "Guys, the coordinates are set. Little Maggie will bring you to us."

Boots patted Ben on the back. "Your little sister is something else, sir."

As Ben started her up, Dylan said, "Sounds like she can move."

Ben agreed, "Let's see what Katie's got in this thing." Ben pushed the accelerator throttle forward; the little vehicle's engine whined, and the trio almost got whiplash. Outside, Tyton rotated the turret and settled in for the ride.

Ben called to his sisters, almost yelling, "We need to get out of here quickly."

"Copy that, Recon 1. We are set to launch when you get here."

Katie lifted off seconds after the others were on board, and Ben and Dylan ran for the cockpit as Boots and Tyton secured the small vehicle. A few moments later, Boots hit a button on the wall, and the little vehicle known as Little Maggie returned to a compartment above. They went to join the others in the cockpit, and Dylan looked at his robotic friend from the copilot's seat. Without a word, Tyton jumped back down the ladder to the defense station. Boots joined him, climbing into the rear laser turret control seat.

The alarms blared from the speakers. Jennifer glanced down to see two blips on the radar.

Dylan spoke, "Fighters! Get us out of here, little lady. Impressive as your ship is, I don't want to see her in action just yet."

"I agree!" Katie pushed a button on the control panel and the small communications sphere outside exploded as they passed it, startling Dylan. "I forgot about that."

The alien fighters closed in on the small craft. Boots fired a few shots in their direction, which made the fighters veer to starboard and Boots kept one of them in the rear gun sight. A short moment later *Vixen* jumped into light speed, narrowly making an escape.

On the bridge of *Tiger's Pride*, TU-413 informed the crew that he had lost communication with *Vixen*. Max looked up, worried.

In Harm's Way

Vixen exited light speed with an uneasy jerk. To Katie, the jump felt different this time. A quick glance at the control panel showed everything was okay. She thought to herself, *It's probably my nerves getting to me.* She immediately contacted the station. "*Big Rock Station*, go to red alert status now, and I want all station defenses online immediately."

The officer in command answered in a nervous voice, "Already have. We thought it best when we lost communications with you guys."

Katie spoke again, "Good. I want all command staff in docking bay one now, and we need a data display module there as well."

"Copy that, Commander."

Jennifer saw her ship moving toward the docking tower. She tapped her headset communication unit to the correct frequency, "Do not dock, *Tiger's Pride*. Stay in a defensive position near the station. Mech 1, get a shuttle and meet me on the station."

The command robot responded with a deep static voice, "Yes, Captain."

As *Vixen* set down on the deck, a small shuttle from *Tiger's Pride* entered the bay close behind. Before it could set down on the deck, its door opened, and Max leaped out, stumbling to the deck. He quickly got his footing and ran to meet his friends. Jennifer hugged him tightly to comfort him.

They joined the nervous crowd as one of the freighter captains standing nearby asked, "What's going on?"

Katie acknowledged him with a glance, and she began to address them. TU-413 and Mech 1 approached; Mech 1 stood next to Jennifer and spoke. "The *Tiger's Pride* is in position." Katie hesitated a moment to allow Boots and his robot aide to get situated. "We have a dangerous situation here. We have discovered an alien civilization within the Orion Nebula. We were detected while on a recon mission and may be in danger of a possible attack."

Dylan shook Ben's arm and whispered in his ear, "Dude, this makes me nervous. Fill me in later. We are going to get the *Saber II* ready. She may be seeing some combat."

Ben shook his head, "Okay, marines."

Dylan snapped back, "Former marines, buddy."

Tyton laid his hand on Ben's shoulder for a second as he followed Dylan, shouldering his laser rifle in the familiar marine style. Ben thought, *Glad those guys are here*. He turned back to listen.

Katie had begun to assess their defensive capabilities. "At best we have the station's defenses and three ships."

Boots whispered in her ear, "Commander, *Pinto* arrived on that freighter that was delayed for repairs."

"Okay, four ships—one is battle cruiser class and three small, well-equipped ships."

The captain who was in charge of the supply fleet spoke up. "Commander, I must correct you. We have nine, possibly ten, ships to help in your defense."

Jennifer asked, a little puzzled, "What do you mean, Captain?"

The captain answered her with pride swelling in his chest. "The five freighters that sit in these docking bays are from Falcon Intergalactic Freight Co. and the best in the business. Your father is security director of our parent company, Falcon Intergalactic, and might I say the best security man I know."

Katie was very interested now; she moved closer. "Continue please."

The freighter captain was not comfortable speaking to crowds, so he asked Ben, Jennifer, and Katie to join him in the other docking bay, so he could explain further. Katie protested, "We don't have time for this."

The man looked at her with a sly little smile. "It is worth your time, little lady."

She reluctantly agreed. She and her siblings followed the cocky captain into docking bay two. He pointed to the closest ship. "This is my ship." He opened a door and pushed a button on the external key pad. The sound of servo motors and metal scrapping against metal filled the bay. Doors on the ship's hull opened and laser turrets emerged.

Dylan looked across the bay at the freighter. He was impressed. "Dang that's awesome!"

Ben had heard him and looked in his direction. Dylan just shrugged his shoulders.

The captain continued, "Mr. H cleared the upgrades after your father convinced him that it was a wise move. He told me the story about pirates attacking his mining operation in the asteroid belt between Mars and Jupiter during the Mars War. He swore he would not be caught off guard again."

Jennifer asked the captain, "Captain, you mentioned possibly ten ships. Where is the tenth one?"

The chubby captain loved this. He said, smiling at them, "*Big Willie* is the tenth."

Katie looked at him, "That old barge?"

He replied. "That old barge has a secret flight deck with twenty-four fighters on it. I'll call for it if you like."

Both women said, "Please!"

Laughing, the captain went to make a request of a friend. Ben told his sisters, "We need to get back to the meeting." They walked toward the door to join the others.

Alien's Face Revealed

While they were in the other bay, Boots and the others had moved to the dining hall.

The meeting had answered many questions and left some unanswered. The images that flickered on the dining hall wall were new and unfamiliar to many in the room. As for the small group that had visited the planet, they were too familiar. After joining the meeting, Dylan sat in the back lost in his thoughts. It bothered him that not all his military and intelligence training had prepared him for what he was feeling. He had been in hot spots before. A human foe he could handle, but the foe he could face soon shook him to his soul. One that was alien and unfamiliar. He looked to his right. He saw his friends sitting there—one human and one robot. He felt a sense of calm come over him because he knew they would have his back.

At the front of the room stood the cyborg he knew as Boots. He noticed his cowboy boots on his feet. He laughed and thought to himself. *He must have put them on when he changed out of the S.E. P.A. suit.* He turned and looked at the two young women sitting close together. He had grown up around them, but today he had developed a great respect for them. They both had talent and smarts. Most women he had met had one or the other not both. Even the way they dressed had impressed him. Their uniforms complied with military regulations, and even their hairstyles were military. Jennifer wore her hair long in a braid, and Katie had a short style. He knew the two men who had the most influence on them growing up. Their father and a friend they called Willie, so no wonder they turned out the way they did. He smiled. He would not hesitate to go into combat with those women. He stared at the massive tiger lying at their feet; he could not help but admire the beauty and strength the beast possessed. He thought about the love and loyalty the tiger showed his human companions. He could not think of a better bodyguard.

Ben shook his friend. "Hey, man, you awake?"

Dylan sat up straight. "Yeah, I'm just thinking about things."

"What things?" Tyton asked.

"Just stuff I got on my mind, nothing worth sharing. What have I missed?" he asked.

Ben shrugged his shoulders. "Not much, just data about the planet. They are calling it Nebula One. The brains up there think those ruins we photographed were not damaged by natural means. They think a bomb of some kind caused their destruction. Those guys have been in a war. They are not sure if it was a planetary one or interplanetary."

Dylan was interested now. He moved a few seats closer.

Boots continued to brief the group. "We are certain that these creatures can fight if they chose to do so. We can assume from the data that they may not be aggressive. Their cities are below the planet's surface with very few structures above ground." He pointed to the image of the ruins. "The ruins are uninhabited, possibly been abandoned for decades. The only structures above the surface are hangars and landing pads. This is if all the other areas on the planet are similar. In addition, they did not pursue the recon group, and they most certainly could have."

A gun sight image appeared behind Boots. The group let out a collective gasp. Katie covered her eyes a brief moment. She spoke, "I am glad I didn't see that. I would have freaked."

Dylan disagreed with her. "I saw you at the controls of your ship; and, girl, you had ice water flowing through your veins."

She blushed at the compliment. "Thanks. I am still glad I didn't see them."

Suddenly alarms screeched all over the station. Jennifer's headset communications unit crackled to life. "Captain, we have three ships approaching about five thousand miles out. At the speed they are approaching, they appear serious."

Jennifer yelled to the group as they headed for the station's command deck. "People, we have incoming hostiles!" Mech 1 looked at his friend and captain, and Jennifer knew what was on his mechanical brain. "No time, big guy. We make our stand here. They will have to fight without us." Jennifer ran from the room heading for the command deck followed closely by her robotic officer and her tiger bodyguard.

Ben ran out the other door screaming every breath into his headset communications unit for his partners to wait. Dylan's voice sounded in his ear, "Dude, you better get here fast. Tyton is steaming for a fight. He practically carried me out of the dang door."

Ben reached the *Saber II* and had to jump into the hatch, just as it lifted off the deck. He yelled up to his friends in the cockpit, "I am in, and I got the gun controls down here."

Dylan yelled back, "Works for me, pal. I am betting I'll have my hands full flying the ship."

Ben laughed. "Well, you better get me good shots."

Dylan sighed. "I'll try."

Just as the *Saber II* rounded the station, *Tiger's Pride* opened fire. Two of the fighters exploded instantly, but the third made it through the laser fire from the larger ship. The *Saber II* streaked by the command deck viewport on its intercept course. Boots followed close in his ship *Pinto*. Dylan's tense voice crackled over the speakers, "We got it!"

The forward laser guns erupted, raining laser fire down upon the attacking craft. A couple of laser bolts found their mark. The small craft shuttered and crashed into the station near the astronomy dome. Ben could see sparks ripple through the downed fighter in his targeting monitor.

Katie spoke to the crew of the *Saber II*, "Return to the station, guys. Sensors indicate the pilot is still alive."

"Roger that Commander. We'll be there in a few." Boots flew in for a closer look before returning to the station.

The victorious trio entered the medical center as the alien pilot was carried in. Dylan and Ben looked down at the fallen pilot as he passed by them. Dylan grabbed Ben by the arm and pulled him out into the hall. Katie noticed Dylan's behavior and went after them. She motioned for her sister to follow. She confronted Dylan, "What's up?"

Dylan leaned against the wall. He could not believe what he was about to say.

"The aliens are Sasquatch!"

The others screamed, "What!"

Ben said, "That old twentieth-century legend?"

"It is not a legend anymore. That creature in there is a Sasquatch. I knew those ships seemed familiar. Earth intelligence found one on Mars in the polar ice cap along with some bones, and also on Earth in the Alaskan wilderness, we found a skeleton in a hidden bunker."

Ben looked angry. "Why have I not heard about this? I am in the alien biological field."

Dylan replied, "Earth's UN covered it up just before the Interstellar Alliance declared independence and I learned about it when I joined intelligence near the end of the war."

Dylan stopped Boots as he approached. "Boots, where did you come from? We did not see you running toward the docking bays."

Boots grinned. "I launched from the maintenance bay. I had my ship, *Pinto*, put there when it arrived. How was my flying?"

"Not bad." Dylan patted his new friend on the back as they turned to follow the others.

The group walked back into the room. Katie spoke as they looked through the glass at the creature on the table, "Well, our aliens have a face now."

A Message of Peace

Boots looked over the translation of the alien transmissions once more to be sure he had translated them correctly. He looked at his aide, TU-413, for assurance. The robot spoke to his boss. "Sir, we have looked over them a dozen times. They are correct."

He rubbed his eyes. They burned from the long hours he had spent looking at the monitor and printouts. For the first time since he had joined the Cyborg Corp., he wished he had opted for cybernetic enhanced eyes. "Come on, TU-413; let's give the boss the news."

The robot rolled along beside his cyborg companion. "Sir, this is good news?"

"Oh yeah, it is good news."

The pair found their commanding officer on a bench outside the medical center. She sat alone thinking. She turned in their direction as they approached. She knew it was Boots by the sound his boots made as he walked in the door. She greeted them, "Hey, Boots. What's up?"

"Commander, I think the attack wasn't approved by whoever is in charge on Nebula One." He handed her the printout. She looked at it and began to read. The words "*Do not attack and return home*" jumped off the paper. The next line was one she had seen before. "*Humans too close*."

Katie scratched her head. "It seems to me the attack was a rogue one. What *do* you think?"

"I think so too."

Katie walked over to a communication panel and made the announcement, "Attention all personnel, the station will be under a yellow alert from this moment on unless a change is needed." A light above her head turned from red to yellow, as all the others on the station had done.

The headset communication unit around her neck crackled to life, and she placed it to her ear. It was her big sister. "Why has the security alert been changed?"

She told her sister to get the gang together for a meeting in her quarters and let the headset communication unit fall back around her neck. She looked back toward the alien patient's room.

"Boots, what are we going to do with him?" She walked down the hall. Her loyal aide and friend followed without saying a word.

A short time later, Katie fell asleep as she relaxed in her favorite chair. Boots noticed she had fallen asleep, so he let her sleep. He thought about the many times the young woman had done that in the past week. "She has been working too hard lately."

The door opened, and he gestured for the small group to be quiet. Ben whispered, "What is up, Boots?"

He looked at them with relief on his face. "Well, TU-413 and I just translated the alien signals we picked up before the attack. It seems those fighter pilots disobeyed orders to return home and made the decision to attack on their own without permission from those in charge."

Dylan said loudly, "Radicals!"

The tiger at his side growled low in his direction.

"Sorry, I hate that type of soldier," he whispered.

The speaker on the desk broke the silence. Boots scrambled to plug his headset communication unit into the desk. "This is Boots. What is it?"

The deck officer apologized and gave his report.

"Sir, we have received a transmission from the planet."

Boots ordered the officer to send it through the translation computer and to get back with him.

The officer exclaimed, "Sir, the message is meant for us, and it isn't scrambled."

He answered the other officer, "Be right there." He unplugged his headset communication unit and headed for the door. "Come on, guys."

Jennifer asked as she followed, "What about Katie?"

"Let her sleep. I'll call her when we find out what's going on."

They all sprinted onto the command deck. The message was replayed for them. "*We do not want war. War is bad. Want to be left alone. Leaders did not give permission for attack.*"

They looked at one another. No one spoke for a few minutes.

Katie startled them when she entered the command center. "Hey, guys! What is going on? I thought we were supposed to meet in my quarters." Boots did not say a word; he reached down and played the recording again. The message filled the quiet room once more.

"*We do not want war. War is bad. Want to be left alone. Leaders did not give permission for attack.*"

Katie just looked down at the speaker. Boots walked over to her. "What do you think, Commander? It is your call."

She looked up. "Can we match the frequency and translation?"

TU-413 responded immediately, "Yes, we can whenever you are ready to start, Commander." Katie gestured to the robot, and he flipped a switch.

She began to speak into the microphone, "Willing to talk, but we will need a few days to get a negotiator here. No one here is skilled in diplomacy. We have one of your pilots. He survived the attack and needed medical attention."

She turned to the group and said, "Well, that's all I can do." She turned to her aide, "Boots, get a diplomat out here. Tell them it's urgent."

He turned to carry out his commander's order. "I am on it."

The next couple of days passed without incident. *Big Willie* had arrived and left since it was not needed. Its captain was disappointed he had missed the action, but he was relieved no one was hurt.

The Interstellar Alliance cruiser exited light speed with a squadron of fighters accompanying it. A request for permission to land came from the lead fighter. "This is Commander Jared, leader of the diplomatic fighter squadron four. The ambassador's ship requests permission to land." The permission to land came almost instantly.

"Permission granted to land in docking bay two."

"Copy that, *Big Rock Science Station.*" Jared, the squad leader, responded.

The small cruiser entered the docking bay with the two lead fighters in close formation beside it. The three ships set down at exactly the same time. It looked like it had been rehearsed to Dylan. He was impressed by his younger brother's piloting skills. Jared stood by his fighter at attention until the diplomatic officials left the bay. He told his companion to see to the other fighters. He walked over to say hello to his big brother.

"Hey, Dylan, I figured you would be right in the middle of something like this."

"Hi there, little man. You looked good in that fighter."

The two men shared a quick hug. The military had made such show of affections uncomfortable to them. Dylan led Jared toward the door. "Let me buy you a drink."

Jared hesitated. "I am on duty."

Dylan chuckled. "Okay, nothing with alcohol."

They laughed and left the docking bay.

A Time for Change

In the late hours of the evening, Jennifer gave the orders for *Tiger's Pride* to move away from the station and into the Orion Nebula. Upon the diplomat's request, the negotiations would take place at a neutral point within the nebula aboard *Tiger's Pride*. A few moments after they had taken up position at the coordinates set by the two parties, a small craft moved out of the darkness with its fighter escorts. It was directed to the landing bay where the negotiations would take place. Jennifer was glad she would not have to leave the bridge. Boots agreed to assist during the proceedings. She sat in her chair and thought about the events of the past week. Her sister was not so calm. Katie paced the floor.

"It will be fine, sis," Jennifer tried to calm her younger sibling.

On the *Big Rock Science Station*, things were quiet with officials gone on *Tiger's Pride*. In docking bay two, a small group of pilots passed the time by playing cards. Ben, Dylan, and Jared did not want to be left out, so they joined them. After few hands, the two brothers left Ben to fend for himself against the flyboys.

"Tyton, look out for our buddy there," Dylan whispered as they left.

Dylan led his little brother over to his fighter and pointed to the decal on the side. Dylan thought it looked out of place on the small craft. It was a heart with a ribbon above it. Jared explained it to his brother proudly, "The heart with Bessie inside is for Mom, and the ribbon with *Momma's Boy* is for me. You see, the guys in flight school called me 'Momma's Boy,' and it stuck, and it seemed appropriate after I graduated to put it on my fighter."

Dylan shook his head. "Works for me; I was just curious. What does Dad think of it?"

The younger brother answered proudly, "Who do you think helped me put it on?"

Back on *Tiger's Pride* after several hours, the order came from the landing bay for the doors to be opened.

Katie looked a little surprised. "It's over already?"

Jennifer stretched and sighed. "I guess so."

Boots' voice came over Katie's headset communication unit, "Commander, the negotiations are over, and our guests are eager to leave. They are extremely shy and withdrawn. They got straight to the point, which made things simple and quick."

The small alien craft exited the landing bay. After it reached a sufficient distance from the larger ship, it jumped to light speed and was gone. Its fighter escorts followed it closely.

Jennifer gave the command for the ship to change course and jump into light speed for its return to the *Big Rock Science Station*. The jump was a short one, and a few moments later, *Tiger's Pride* was back in position near the station. In docking bay two, the deck officer yelled to the men sitting on the deck, "Hey, guys! We got a shuttle coming in. Game is over."

A pilot yelled, "Dang, I was winning!" The others laughed as they picked up their stuff.

Jared yelled to his pilots, "Look sharp, guys; the bigwigs are coming in."

As the shuttle landed, a group of reporters ran into the docking bay with hover camera robots floating near each reporter.

The head diplomat stopped at the top of the ramp to address the crowd. "The negotiations were short and to the point. The inhabitants of the planet known as Nebula One have approved the name we gave it."

A reporter from Mars News Station 1 asked the first question, "Are these creatures the legendary Sasquatch?"

"Yes, the creature from the twentieth-century legend was one of their races."

The lone Earth reporter spoke up, "What are some of the things agreed upon?"

"First of all, we will retain only this station. The Nebula One inhabitants will control the Orion Nebula."

Protests filled the bay.

"I understand your disappointment. During our talks, we learned much about them. Their civilization is rebuilding. They have earned the rights to the mentioned territory and the right to be left alone."

Someone yelled from the crowd, "Why?"

The diplomat continued to explain, "About two hundred years ago, the Orion Nebula was home to two civilized worlds. Both were equal in technology. Relations broke down and war ensued. The Nebula One inhabitants won the war by completely obliterating the opposing race. Their victory came with a price. Loss of life was great on their world. All that remains of the civilization are a few sub terrain compounds they use as cities. Next thing, any human entering the nebula will forfeit his right to protection from the Earth or the Interstellar Alliance. Their society is strict."

One of the pilots spoke up. "What about the Sasquatch pilot?"

"The pilot we captured here will not live to see another day. Trust me; it is in our best interest to honor this treaty. It will be posted at each entrance to the docking bays on this station. For those who are thinking of trying something stupid, I strongly advise against it. This station will become an embassy to monitor activity near the nebula. Thank you for your time. All the documents will be made public in the morning."

One last question came from the crowd. "Will Earth be allowed to send an ambassador here?"

"We will be in talks with Earth officials soon about that."

Jared gestured for his pilots to escort the officials through the crowd.

Katie and Jennifer had remained on *Tiger's Pride*. Katie wanted to talk over some things with her sister because she had a decision to make. They went to Jennifer's quarters and talked until morning. Before anyone was stirring on the station, Katie returned to her office, and after about an hour or so, she called in Boots. Boots sat in disbelief as Katie spoke, "Boots, things have changed here very quickly. The politicians of the Interstellar Alliance have taken away from me what I worked years to build. They feel the need turn my station into an embassy for diplomats. I signed up for a research station not an embassy. Here is my letter of resignation. I officially turn the *Big Rock Science Station* over to you."

It is time to make a change, Katie thought to herself as she walked to get her things.

Farewells and a New Beginning

Tiger's Pride drifted near the station waiting for her captain.

The whole gang gathered in docking bay two. Ben, Dylan, and Tyton talked to Jared. They were scheduled to be the first to depart. Boots ran into the bay, so he would not miss saying good-bye to his new friends.

Dylan grabbed his hand first. "Well, old man, I guess this is good-bye."

As Boots pulled his hand back, he said, "Nice to have met you, Marine."

Tyton leaned in and shook Boots' hand.

"Later, Tyton. Take care of these two."

Tyton did not speak, only nodded his head. It was Ben's turn to say good-bye.

Boots shook his hand and said, "See you around, young man. Really been nice knowing you."

Ben smiled and said, "Been nice knowing you too, Boots."

Boots waved as he walked away. "I need to get back to work."

Boots passed Jennifer as she and Max entered the bay. She grabbed him and gave him a hug.

"Good-bye. Glad to have met you."

Jennifer spoke into his ear before pulling away. "I am glad I met you too. See you."

Boots rubbed Max on the head as he walked away. "See you, Max. You take care of Jennifer."

Boots saw Katie standing in the doorway. A lump swelled up in his throat, and he thought to himself, *The hardest good-bye stands right there.* Tears had filled his eyes before he even said a word. Katie was sobbing also. He hugged his long-time friend. "I'll miss you so much, Katie. It will not be the same here without you. We built this rock together."

Katie fought back the sobs so she could speak. "I am going to miss you too. I couldn't have done it without you." Boots pulled away rubbing tears from his face, and he did not look back as he walked away. She yelled to him, "Take care of my baby, okay?"

Boots turned and smiled. "You better believe I will, Commander."

Katie lost it. She turned and saw her big sister waiting for her. She ran to her, and Jennifer tried to comfort her. They turned and walked to say good-bye to the group. By the time Katie had gotten her sobbing under control a little, they reached the *Saber II*.

Ben, Jennifer, and Katie hugged in their usual group hug. Ben spoke first, "Well, ladies, I guess it's time to go. I wish we had more time, but I have to file a report on this deal out here. Then who knows where." Katie wiped a tear from his face thinking a tear was rare for Ben. He seldom showed emotions. She thought to herself the events of the past few days had brought them closer.

Dylan gave each of the girls a quick hug good-bye and said to them, "You ladies take it easy. It's been fun."

"Take care, Dylan," Katie told him.

Jennifer punched him on the shoulder. "Later. You take care, Dylan."

Tyton waived to the girls as he left the group to get the ship ready. Katie and Jennifer said bye to Tyton.

Dylan looked to his brother and gave him a hug. He whispered, "See you later, Momma's Boy."

They laughed. He waved once more as he turned to go up the ramp. He looked back, seeing Max standing at Jennifer's side. He yelled back, "See you, Max."

He went inside. Ben gave them one more hug. He gave Jared a hug and whispered, "Watch those flyboys you hang around with; they'll take your money."

They laughed.

Jennifer blurted out, "What's up with the whispering?"

Jared laughed again. "It's just guy stuff."

Ben grinned as the door shut.

The ones left standing on the deck moved out of the way. The *Saber II* lifted off the deck and moved toward the door. A moment later, it was gone.

The ladies placed their arms around Jared, their younger cousin. Katie asked, "Walk us to my ship?"

They walked arm-in-arm toward the docking bay next door. Katie's ship looked like it was sad. Katie thought, *Must be the emotions messing with my head.* They stood beside *Vixen* silently for a few moments, each finding it hard to say good-bye.

Jennifer broke the silence. "Well, take care of yourself." She gave her cousin a big hug. She shed a few tears as she backed up to give Katie a turn to say her good-bye.

Katie grabbed Jared so hard it took his breath. "See you, Jared. Take care." She tuned to join her sister with tears filing her eyes.

Max walked over and nudged Jared, and he was startled a little. He rubbed the tiger on the head. "See you, big guy."

Jennifer smiled. "Come on, Max."

The door shut behind them.

Jared turned, trying not to let his sadness show. He thought to himself as he walked away, *I am just getting here, and everyone else is leaving. That stinks! Comes with a pilot's life I guess.*

Katie piloted *Vixen* out of the docking bay for the last time. Moments later, they were setting down in the landing bay aboard *Tiger's Pride*. They strolled down *Vixen*'s rear loading ramp. They were sad. Jennifer looked at her little sister and asked, “Where to? It is your choice.”

Katie smiled, “Let’s go see Dad.”

“Good idea.” Jennifer tapped her headset communication unit. “Mech 1, tell those guys up there to set a course for Jupiter.”

Moments later as they entered the bridge, *Tiger’s Pride* made a perfect jump to light speed. Jennifer sat in her chair and waved for a chair for her sister. Two of the bridge crew secured a chair to the deck beside the captains’ chair. The sisters looked at each other and said at the same time, “Daddy, here we come.”

Part 2

Panthers Return

Explosive Arrival

Tiger's Pride entered the familiar space around the Planet Jupiter. Mech 1 turned to announce their arrival. "Captain, we have entered the Jupiter system, and preliminary scans have not detected your father's station."

Jennifer looked at the monitor in the command console at her side and pushed a button. The sensor scan of the system showed little activity around the gas giant, and she thought aloud, "It is probably on the other side." As she looked at the planet in the viewport, she put on her headset to call her sister. "Katie, we are here. Katie, are you there?"

Katie was in the hangar bay, where she had spent most of the trip. She had passed the time tinkering around her ship, *Vixen*. Max nudged Katie to get her attention. She looked up from her work on her beloved small-tracked transport, Little Maggie. "What do you want now?"

Jennifer's voice crackled from her toolbox. "Hey are you there? Katie!"

She picked up her headset to answer her sister. "Yeah, I'm here. What's up, Jen?"

"I thought you might want to know we have arrived at Jupiter." Katie ran for the hangar's exit.

A few moments later, Katie stepped into the corridor behind the bridge, and the sound of an alarm caught her attention. She ran to see what was happening. She heard Jennifer and Mech 1 talking. When she reached her sister's side, she sat silently. The alarm stopped as Jennifer spoke. "The power reactor on that mining station is about to explode!" She pointed out the viewport, so Katie would know which station she was referring to.

Katie stood and looked a out the viewport and then back to her sister. Seeing worry in her younger sister's eyes, Jennifer immediately spoke. "That isn't Dad's station."

Katie felt better but still was tense about what was going on.

A blip on the monitor at Jennifer's side caught Katie's eye. "Hey, guys, a ship is launching from the station." Before anyone could respond to her comment, the space station exploded violently in the Jupiter sky. Katie put her hand on Max's back as she gasped. The tiger nudged her to comfort her.

Jennifer asked, "Did the ship make it out?"

The crewmember at the sensor console spoke. "Yes, Captain, but it was struck by a piece of debris. I'll scan for life signs."

The young man pulled the sensor pylon to him.

As Jennifer sat down, she noticed a familiar signal coming from the damaged ship. She gasped and grabbed Katie's arm. "That is Bethany's ship."

They looked out of the viewport worriedly to see the ship drifting powerless in space. Without looking at his captain, Mech 1 gave an order to dispatch a tug drone to pick up the ship. Jennifer thanked her mechanical friend as she ran for the door on her way to the hangar bay. Without saying a word, Katie and Max followed close behind.

The trio rode the elevator in silence. Jennifer thought about the last time she had seen her best friend. It had been back before she had left for the job with Falcon Intergalactic. They had buried her kitten, Cream. Bethany, it seemed, had always been there for her. Katie put her arms around her older sister to reassure her. Jennifer whispered a prayer, "Lord, please let my best friend Bethany be okay."

The door opened, and Jennifer ran out with Katie struggling to keep up.

Katie caught up with her sister as the tug drone lifted the battered S-17 Raider, known as *Kit-Cat*, up into the hangar bay. Even before the ship had been placed on the deck, Mech 1 had arrived. He instructed the rescue and medical teams in what needed to be done. He then joined his captain, Jennifer, who reluctantly held back. Mech 1 reassured her. "Your friend is alive, and we will have her out of the ship momentarily. The ship's life support was damaged." Jennifer was relieved but not much. She still was concerned for her friend, and a tear ran down her cheek.

Katie tugged at her sister's arm. "Come on, sis. Let's go up and wait in the medical center. We cannot do anything here." Jennifer reluctantly agreed as she looked back at the mangled craft on the deck.

A short time later, Jennifer's friend slept in a medical center bed. "She has minor bumps and bruises. Also her lungs were damaged slightly from the smoke, which had filled her ship," the medical robot said as he made his report on his patient's condition.

Jennifer asked if she could see Bethany. The med robot answered, "Yes, but for a little while. We need to get her into a rejuvenation chamber as soon as possible."

With a smile on her face, Jennifer agreed and headed for the door to her friend's room. She looked back at her sister. Katie smiled. Max started to follow, but Katie pulled his tail to stop him.

"Go on. We will look in on her later."

Max looked up. "Ouch! I hate when you guys do that."

Katie knelt and whispered, "Let's give them a little while."

He growled a low response in agreement.

The friends hugged when Jennifer reached the bedside. They spoke at the same time. "Good to see you."

Jennifer wiped a tear from her cheek. "You were almost killed out there. What are you doing here?"

As she rose up in her bed, Bethany groaned in pain. She smiled and avoided her friend's question for now.

"I'm tougher than that; you know that, girl."

Jennifer sighed. "Maybe so, but you are not super woman."

The friends spoke for a few minutes until the med robot that had come to take Bethany to the rejuvenation chamber interrupted them.

Jennifer hugged her friend and started to leave. "I'll be on the bridge."

Bethany looked around the medical robot to her friend at the door. "I'll be up there when I get out of here. Girl, we need to talk."

Jennifer waved to her friend as she left.

Katie met her older sister in the hall near the main elevators. "How is she?"

Jennifer answered with a smile and a laugh, "She will be okay. She thinks she is super woman though."

The sisters walked arm-in-arm to the elevator. "Come on; let's go and see if Mech 1 knows what happened out there."

Katie looked at her and said, "I know what happened."

Jennifer looked curious. "What?"

Laughing, Katie followed her big sister into the elevator. "It was an explosive arrival; that's what."

The elevator door shut.

Another Adventure

The tension that had greeted *Tiger's Pride*'s crew upon arrival in the system had lessened a bit after a couple hours. In its place was confusion and worry.

Her captain, Jennifer, and her younger sister had become worried because their father was not in the system. His company's officials did not know where he was or did not want to say. Jennifer paced around the bridge, causing her tiger companion, Max, to become nervous. Katie could see this was affecting the crew and approached her. "Jennifer, would you go check on Bethany?"

She smiled and agreed. "She should be out of the rejuvenation chamber by now." She silently strolled out of the bridge.

Her friend was not in the med center. Her treatment was complete, so the medical staff had released her. Someone said she had received a message and went to her ship to check on something.

Jennifer heard voices coming from *Kit-Cat*'s cabin as she approached. She wondered who she could be talking to and went inside to investigate. She caught the end of a conversation with someone with a mechanical voice. "I'll let you go. See you when you arrive."

Jennifer kicked something. Her friend turned quickly, startled. Jennifer jumped back because Bethany had pulled her gun. After catching her breath, she noticed the tear in her friend's eyes. "Oh my God, Bethany are you okay?"

Bethany wiped the tear away and spoke in a crackling voice, "Remember, I said we needed to talk."

Jennifer answered, "Yeah, I do. What's going on?"

Bethany grabbed Jennifer's hand and pulled her out of the door. "Let's find Katie. She needs to hear this too."

A short while later the two had joined the others. Katie was working in the bridge conference room. Mech-1 and Max had joined her shortly before Jennifer and Bethany. Jennifer asked her friend to explain what was going on. "What is up?"

Bethany motioned for Mech 1 to come in the room. The large robot moved from where he had been standing in the doorway. She shut the door and began to speak. "What I am about to say isn't something you will want to hear." Tears filled her eyes. "Willie is dead."

Katie yelled, "What? Are you serious?"

Before she received an answer, she knew it was true. Katie began to cry, and her sister hugged her to comfort her. Jennifer was finding it hard to be reassuring because she was hurting just as bad as her sister. Katie thought of her dad's best friend. She had called him Willie since she was a child.

Attempting to stay composed, Bethany spoke, "I am sorry. I do not know how to say this." Bethany stood up, cursing. "I cannot explain, so I'll show you this. What I am showing you can never leave this room."

"What is going on?" Jennifer and Katie spoke together.

Without looking at them, she put a small disk into the viewer. "Listen to this."

A masked figure appeared on the screen.

Suddenly the door opened and an officer started to enter, but Mech 1 stopped him and pushed him out the door. A moment later, he returned and locked the door. Bethany started the message once again.

"Agent Delta, I am glad you are okay. Things have just turned serious. A few hours ago, I received a signal from Mr. H's life band signaling he was dead. A few weeks ago, he and I programmed it to send me a signal upon his death. He felt the people in the alliance we were investigating would kill us if they discovered our mission."

Katie interrupted. "How did he die?"

Bethany told the small group that she had met with the man they knew as Uncle Willie and who she knew as Mr. H on the mining station that had exploded earlier.

"He was on that station?"

"Yes, he was," Bethany said, trying not to show sadness. "I did not know he had not made it off the station until I got this message. That is all I can say for now."

Jennifer became angry and stood to confront her friend. "What do you mean that is all?"

Bethany stood her ground. "It is complicated, and many people could be killed like your mom."

Jennifer pushed her friend into the chair behind her. "What did you say?"

Katie jumped up to catch Max. The tiger sensed the conflict and wanted to protect his companion. He turned and roared loudly as Katie put her hand on his back. The others turned to see what had happened.

Jennifer in her anger had not noticed Max was getting tense from the activity going on around him. She slid across the table and knelt in front of him. "Max, it is okay; calm down."

The confused and worried tiger licked the tears from her cheek as she hugged him. She whispered in his ear, "Big guy, get out of here and take a walk. I'll be okay."

Jennifer stood and apologized to her friend, who only nodded.

Her tiger companion left the room reluctantly. Mech 1 looked at his captain. "Go with him. He may get into trouble."

He followed the tiger out of the room and caught up with him just as he almost knocked a technician robot over as he left the bridge. A crewmember close to them jumped out of the way. Mech-1 stopped briefly to help the robot regain its balance.

Back in the conference room, tension grew.

"Bethany, you going to tell us what's going on?"

Bethany stood straightening her flight suit. "All I can say is your mother's death is tied into all this somehow. I do not know all the details, but Mr. H did. I was supposed to meet him in a couple days for a briefing."

Katie spoke up. "What are you going to do now?"

"I am meeting with his agent," Bethany said.

Jennifer sat down and sighed. She thought aloud, "The guy in the message."

Hearing what Jennifer said, Katie asked, "Who is that guy?"

Bethany spoke as she turned to remove the data disk from the viewer. "His name is Panther, and he works for Falcon Intergalactic as a covert agent."

Katie asked puzzled, "He is a covert agent? Why do they need a covert agent?"

Bethany replied to her question with a little smile. "Your dad felt it was a good security measure."

Jennifer sat quietly for a while and spoke, "We will take you to your meeting with him."

Bethany disagreed, "No, I cannot let you do that."

"Well, girl, how are you getting there? Did you look at your ship when you were down there earlier?"

Laughing, Bethany said, "You are right, but I hate getting you girls involved."

"Girl, we are involved already."

The trio hugged and laughed, relieving the tension that had a hold on the group for the past half hour.

Jennifer asked her friend where they would be going. She gave her the coordinates for a sector of the asteroid belt. The trio left the room for the bridge. As they left the conference room, Mech 1 and Max returned. Jennifer spoke to her robot friend to tell him what was happening. She started to shout out the coordinates to the helm officer, but Bethany stopped her, whispering in her ear. "We do not want many people knowing where we are going."

Jennifer agreed and walked over to set the coordinates herself. She entered a security code and then the coordinates. The helm officer returned and looked at the coordinates display out of habit only to see flashing dots.

As *Tiger's Pride* moved away from Jupiter, Jennifer received a message from the mining company's office station. The person sending the message said her father had gone on a trip for company business and would call them later. She leaned over to whisper in Bethany's ear. "Can we trust this guy Panther?"

Bethany's reply was, "Oh yeah, we can trust him. I guarantee that."

Katie looked out toward the closest station and thought aloud. "Where is Daddy?"

Bethany smiled a sly little smile.

Jennifer gave the order to make the jump to light speed and walked to sit in her chair. Holding on to her sister's arm, she said, "I guess we stumbled into another adventure."

The younger sibling smiled as the ship made the jump into light speed.

A Light on the Truth

The trip to the asteroid belt was uneventful. *Tiger's Pride* arrived at the coordinates Bethany had given them. But as Jennifer looked out the viewport, she could not see anything besides rocks. An alarm signaled that the exact coordinates had been reached. A puzzled officer spoke. "Captain, the navigation computer indicates we have arrived at the right place." Jennifer nodded as a sign of thanks toward him. She looked at her friend and shrugged her shoulders. The young security agent smiled and entered a code on the console keypad. The signal she sent caused one of the nearby asteroids to make precise movements, causing the ship's sensors to sound an alarm. Jennifer pushed a button on a nearby panel to silence it.

Jennifer asked, "What is up, Bethany?" The answer to her question was a gesture out the view port. Jennifer saw a large red light flashing on a structure built in the rock, and she thought to herself, *Old mining station, that's cool. The asteroid belt is littered with them.*

Mech 1 turned and asked his captain what they should do, and she turned. "It is your call, Bethany."

"Send no radio signal. Just follow the light signals."

The helm officer looked at her puzzled, and she motioned for him to move.

The officer looked at Jennifer, who made a gesture for him to oblige her, but added, "This is my ship. You scratch it; I'll scratch you."

Bethany interrupted her, "Chill, girl, I got it."

Jennifer nervously watched as her friend flew the ship. As she watched, her nervousness turned to amazement. Her longtime friend handled the helm like a pro as she docked with the old station.

Katie broke her silence. "I didn't know you could handle a large craft like this."

Bethany winked at her smaller friend. "Hang with me awhile; you will see I am full of surprises. Come on, girls, let's get this adventure started."

The sisters were curious and followed her, excited. Their companions Max and Mech 1 joined them. The small group exited the airlock and was pleasantly surprised. Katie saw them first and yelled.

"Ben! What are you doing here?"

He hugged his little sister as he started to answer, but Dylan nudged him. Therefore, he just said, "Later, sis. You two will find out soon enough."

Dylan spoke and motioned for them to follow. "Come on this way. Be careful; this station is a little old."

"Is this place safe?" Mech 1 asked, concerned for his companions.

Dylan smiled with his familiar sly smile.

Ben answered, "Yes, it is safe, just old and dirty."

The group walked down the hallway. Mech 1 and Tyton exchanged greetings as they followed. Ben whispered to Dylan as the led the others through the station. "I thought Dad wanted to keep them out of it?"

His partner nudged him to be quiet.

"Things have changed, and Panther feels we need to move up our plans."

Katie had overheard them and glanced at them, a little confused.

Jennifer noticed her look and asked, "What is wrong?"

Katie just shook her head.

Moments later, the group reached the meeting room and was greeted by the mysterious man known as Panther. He spoke very little and motioned for them to sit. Ben was close to Bethany and dusted her chair for her. The gesture did not go unnoticed. As he sat beside Dylan and Tyton, both spoke in unison: "What a stud."

Ben snapped back quickly, "You guys shut up."

Jennifer and Katie had noticed as well and flashed Bethany a smile.

Jennifer whispered, "Girl, you guys got something going on."

Bethany, annoyed with the comment, yelled out, "No!"

Panther looked at her, any expression on his face hidden behind his helmet. Bethany blushed as the others laughed.

Panther stood to get the meeting started. "Some of you know about what is going on, and the rest will soon know. A serious situation is developing rapidly in the Interstellar Alliance. The source of which started even before the Mars War. It was an incident that affected all of you seated before me now."

A voice from a speaker broke in, "Panther, I will tell them."

He turned to answer the voice. "I agree sir. I think it would be best they hear this from you." Pulling up a chair, Panther flipped a switch and the dusty view screen came to life. The image of their father appeared.

Katie screamed, "Hello, Dad!"

Benny returned his daughter's greeting and continued to address the small group. "I am sorry if I sound cold, but the situation is real serious. Girls, I did not want to get you two involved so soon. The death of my best friend calls for immediate action."

Katie spoke quietly, with a grief-filled heart. "Uncle Willie."

Jennifer held her hand because she noticed the pain in her sister's voice.

"He was killed because he had discovered that officials in the government were behind your mom's death."

Bethany asked, "Wasn't the group known as ARES responsible for her death as well as Max's mother and namesake Professor Maxamillion?"

Benny spoke once more to answer her. "Yes, Agent Delta, the terrorist group was responsible, but it was officials in colonial government who had funded the operation. Their motives in starting the war with Earth were not noble, but were based on greed. After the war, those responsible quickly seized power.

"The corruption has spread like a cancer. Our late friend discovered it through his company dealings with the government. It ultimately led to his death. I plan to do something. Panther and I have discussed plans to attack an Interstellar facility or possibly an official."

Ben spoke up, "Dad, wouldn't that make us terrorists?"

He answered his son's question as a father would a son. "They threw the first punches. I have always taught you all to not start a fight, but stand up for yourselves."

Ben replied, "Works for me. I am in."

The others quickly agreed.

Benny addressed Panther, who had been sitting quietly off to the side. "Panther, determine which plan would be best suited to personnel available. We need to move quickly on this. Oh, and take care of my kids."

He answered, "You can count on me, sir. I think they will be okay and can handle themselves. See you soon."

Katie and Jennifer shouted good-bye to their father. His image disappeared as the screen went blank.

Panther spoke to the group. "Will you all excuse me? I need to do some things. Be ready. Things are going to get tense from now on."

The group left the room as he turned to a communication panel.

Katie spoke, "Well, we have some light on the truth." The others agreed with the youngest member of the group.

An Unwelcome Homecoming

A few emotion-filled days later, a meeting was called, and the small group gathered in the station's conference room. Panther stood to inform the group of what would happen in the next few days.

"A target has been selected, and a recon group has confirmed it as what earlier reports say it is. We do not want to harm any innocent people. The target is the headquarters of the terrorist group ARES."

The silence was shattered by mumbles from everyone. Panther understood their anxiety, but time was short. "People, we must get ready. Jennifer and Katie will pilot us in and out. I heard about your skills, little lady."

Katie blushed and said, "In *Vixen*, I hope."

"Dylan and Bethany will lead the ground action."

Jennifer protested, "I am not staying on the ship this time."

Panther nodded to her and agreed. "Everyone will be involved, and we will need your help. I just want you two to know that your main duty is getting us in and out. Our success depends on that."

The meeting continued for a short time, filled with intense preparations.

The group gathered in the dilapidated docking bay a short time later. Jennifer found herself once again in disagreement with her tiger companion. "Max, no, you cannot go. I am not in charge. I can take care of myself."

After a short intense discussion, the tiger conceded. "Left behind again," he complained through his cybernetic device. The two joined Mech 1. Jennifer instructed him to take *Tiger's Pride* to the *Big Rock* station, which had been designated as the meeting place after the mission. The robotic aide left her to carry out her orders. He looked back for Max and saw he was saying good-bye to the others, so he waited. A minute later, Max ran by Jennifer to join his robotic friend.

She touched him on the head and said, "Love you, big guy."

With a static-filled response, he said, "Love you too. Good-bye and good luck, friend."

She joined the group as Ben piloted Katie's ship *Vixen* into the hangar. Katie looked at her and then looked back to watch her brother maneuver her ship around the abandoned equipment. "Max was complaining about not being able to go with us."

Jennifer replied to her comment. "Yeah, he worries about me."

Jennifer looked around the group and noticed that Tyton was not there. She also saw two others she did not recognize and tugged at Bethany's arm. "Who are they?"

With a sly smile, she replied, "Oh, I called in some explosives experts from Saturn. The older one is Charles, and the young one is Kenny."

Noticing the resemblance, Jennifer asked, "Are they related?"

Bethany looked up from her backpack. "Yeah, they are brothers. That is what makes them good at what they do. I have seen them work. It is like each knows what the other is thinking." She also added, "Do not worry; you can trust them. They are not big Alliance fans."

Panther called for the group to board the ship. As they boarded, Jennifer asked Ben and Dylan where Tyton was. Dylan answered her, "He will be piloting the *Saber II*." Seeing the confusion on his sister's face, Ben pulled her to the side. "Jennifer, we will be staying on Mars. I am going to get my research material from work. I am betting I won't get another chance."

Jennifer understood why her brother had told her. He did not want her to worry when he did not return to the landing zone.

Jennifer left her brother and joined Katie in the cockpit. Bethany and Panther accompanied them there.

Panther spoke with his familiar static voice. "Whenever you are ready, ladies, we can go."

Katie fired up the engines and flew the small ship into the asteroid-filled space beyond the hangar door. Jennifer looked out the window at her ship and noticed that it too had begun to move away from the station. Something else caught her eye. It was Ben and Dylan's ship, *Saber II.* Tyton saw her looking out the window and rocked his ship, as if to wave good-bye. Jennifer waved and smiled at him.

Katie piloted her ship around the nearby rocks and positioned it for the light speed jump. With the *Saber II* along side, *Vixen* jumped into light speed. A moment later, the *Saber II* jumped. The mission had begun.

A short time later Katie looked out at her home planet Mars. She looked around at the others and said, "This is going to one be unwelcome homecoming." Everyone present agreed.

An Eye for an Eye

Katie piloted *Vixen* into the Mars atmosphere, careful to be casual. They did not want to draw any more attention than necessary. She flipped a switch, and the ship's propellers engaged, causing the flight to become uncommonly quiet for a spacecraft.

Panther commented, "Your father's design is impressive. I heard about it, but seeing it in action is something."

The sisters exchanged a glance and a smile. Bethany punched a few numbers on the navigation console pad, causing an alarm to sound. Katie and Jennifer made the necessary flight adjustments, and it silenced.

The small ship flew silently toward a remote part of Mars, where another operative was waiting with a couple of small hover scouts. Katie expressed disappointment that she would not be able to use her little tracked vehicle, Little Maggie. She did not push the issue because she had driven one of the small vehicles and knew they would be faster.

After a short time, they arrived at their destination, and Bethany tapped her on the shoulder and pointed at the waiting vehicles. The propellers made the landing almost unnoticeable to the passengers in the cabin below.

As the group stood and put on their helmets ready to exit the ship, Ben hit a switch to turn off the lights, causing the emergency light to come on. They would illuminate their exit, but lessen the chances of detection. Dylan and the brothers from Saturn began to roll out the camouflage cover, which they planned to throw over the ship. Katie and Jennifer set the ship to standby mode. The mission on Nebula One had proved that it would help in a quick launch. Jennifer glanced out the window at Panther and Bethany talking to the stranger. She noticed that he was wearing a suit similar to Panther's suit, only newer.

The group quickly prepared to depart and mounted the hover scouts. Jennifer leaned to whisper in her friend's ear, "Who was that?"

Bethany hesitated but knew she could trust Jennifer, so she answered, "That is Commander Lee Hughes. He is my boss back at Saturn Colony. He is Willie's nephew and wanted to help. He is extremely angry about his uncle's death and wanted to come along, but Panther would not allow him to." Jennifer looked back at the commander, feeling sad. Willie after all was a friend to her, but was family to him.

Katie sat back in her seat with her eyes closed, thinking. *I am glad we are using these things. Little Maggie would have beaten the crap out of us.*

Jennifer sat beside her, lost in her own thoughts. She looked out at the other craft, and her eyes met Ben's eyes. She had never seen an expression on his face like that before. She found it difficult to read his emotions.

The ride seemed quicker than it was. Dylan and Panther maneuvered the small crafts behind a hill near one of the compound's secondary airlocks. They jumped out and knelt by the vehicles for a quick briefing. Dylan signaled to them to activate their protective suits' stealth settings. The S.E.P.A. suit had been designed to prevent detection by life sign sensors and other detection devises and had worked perfectly on Nebula One. He thought, *Another one of Ben's impressive inventions.*

That was why he agreed to help Ben retrieve his stuff from his lab. The last thing he wanted was his friend to lose his work to the Interstellar Alliance.

Charles and Kenny had already begun placing explosive charges at the airlocks around the complex, which would destroy them. If things went as planned, this would cause loss of the atmosphere inside the remote facility, sealing everyone inside buildings and killing the poor unlucky souls outside. The others waited patiently for the brothers to return. The three women in the group sat together going over details. They were in charge of planting explosives at the ammunitions storage building, while the others would concentrate on the hangar and any ships they can.

The Saturn boys, which Panther called them, returned and signaled to Panther that all outer charges were set, and he motioned for the others to join him. As he placed the electronic lock picker on the door, he tapped Bethany's visor. She blushed because she had forgotten to darken the tint. Before it darkened, Jennifer and Katie caught a glimpse of her smile. The door opened as the device hit the correct code. The small group moved in, with Dylan and Ben leading while Panther took up the rear. Ben gave his sisters the thumbs-up sign as he followed his ex-marine friend toward the hangar. Jennifer saw Bethany and their mysterious leader exchange hand signals. For the second time since meeting him, she got a sense of a connection between them. Bethany motioned for them to follow and they did. The trio headed for their target as Panther ran to catch up with the guys. The other two remained at a position near the hovercraft, because they needed to remain outside for successful detonation of the explosive at the airlocks.

Placement of the explosives at the hangar went without incident, and the group had returned to the airlock, but at the ammunition shed, things were a little tense. A guard on patrol had caused the trio of young women to seek cover. The guard did not see them. Jennifer motioned for them to come out, but at that moment, a second person turned the corner. Jennifer recognized him instantly. She remembered him. He was the ARES spokesperson whom she had seen on the news that had taken credit for the attack that had killed her mother and friend. She remembered him gloating and smiling about it. Anger overtook her, and she fired her gun, hitting him dead in the face. As he fell, she cursed at him, something she seldom did. Seeing the dead man on the ground made Jennifer freeze. Bethany grabbed her hand and pulled her friend after her. Katie was far ahead, almost to the airlock. Ben and Dylan had taken positions to cover them if needed. As the women ran for the airlock, Panther signaled everyone through, and they ran and jumped behind a nearby rock formation. Before he made it out, explosions started throughout the complex. The plan succeeded, and the loss of atmosphere caused everyone to be sealed in the buildings.

The group made a quick departure. Ben and Dylan headed for the *Saber II*, waiting somewhere on Mars. Commander Hughes had sent someone for Charles and Kenny, and they sped off toward a transport eastward. The others made their way to the waiting *Vixen*.

Katie looked back towards the domed structure as it went completely dark. She thought to herself. *The explosives we set must have done more damage than expected.* A short time later, *Vixen* lifted off the surface as the commander from Saturn skimmed the surface on his way back to his own ship. Panther went to the communications console to send a message. He politely allowed Jennifer to pass as she left the cockpit. She sat by Bethany, and feeling safe in the cabin, she removed her helmet, revealing tear-filled eyes. She whispered to Bethany so the others would not hear, "Thanks for helping me back there."

Bethany smiled at her. "We always said we would have each other's back didn't we? Don't mention it."

As she wiped tears from her face, she explained what happened. "He was the guy we saw on the news bragging about what ARES had done, how they had killed mom and my friend, Professor Maxamillion. I was overcome with anger, and before I knew it, that person was dead. I never killed anything or anyone before."

Bethany put her arms around her friend and said, "It says in the Bible an eye for eye. Look at it this way, you were owed an eye, and today you got it."

A Moment of Reflection

Boots sat in his office on the *Big Rock* science station waiting for the message to be transferred to him. The bridge communications officer said it had come on a secure frequency and needed a code from him to descramble. A few short moments passed, and the screen was filled with a familiar logo. He recognized it immediately and knew who it was. He thought aloud, "It is Panther."

Hearing what his partner said, TU-413 rolled over in his utility pod. Boots glanced up and returned to the screen to watch the message. He pushed a button, and Panther's image filled the screen. He could not help but notice the familiar surroundings, so he listened close.

"Major, I am sorry to be sending this message, but the situation in the Interstellar Alliance has become serious enough that General Benny Graham has called for the Panthers to take action. General William Hughes has been killed. He and I were investigating top officials in the Interstellar Alliance and confirmed that they were funding the terrorist group ARES when they killed General Graham's wife back before the Mars War. I cannot go into details now, but I am in route to your station now, as well as other allies. I can say the war with Earth was not inspired by a noble cause, but one nurtured by greed. You must take control of the station. I understand that the Interstellar Alliance ambassador is General Hughes' niece. Show her this information. I will speak with you when I get there."

Boots looked over the data attached to Panther's message. Little that he read surprised him, for he had mistrust of the Interstellar Alliance since the war. TU-413 spoke, "Sir, this is serious, isn't it? What are you going to do?"

Boots sat quietly for a moment, then removed the insignia from his vest and put it on the desk. Walking toward the door, he instructed his robotic partner to tell the ambassador he needed to speak with her. TU-413 carried out his order without question.

A short time later Sarah opened the door to Boots' office. She stopped just a step inside because Boots greeted her in his Panther combat uniform. "Come in, Sarah, we need to talk."

He handed her a piece of paper, and she nervously took it and sat down as she began reading. Boots spoke as she read, "I am taking control of this station, and I hope that you will understand, as I believe you will."

The young woman stood as she looked up from the paper with horror on her face. "I promise you, sir. I will not give you any trouble, and my security personnel will not as well."

Tears began to roll down her cheeks as she turned to leave. "We will talk later, Boots. I need to be alone now."

Sarah grabbed her ambassadorial pendent, jerking it from her neck and letting it fall to the floor. The door shut behind the grief-stricken young woman as she left.

Boots leaned back in his chair and closed his eyes. In his mind's eye, he could see his late friend, William standing over him with the large gas planet of Jupiter behind him, lifting a bulkhead off him during the space battle. Mr. H had been his commanding officer. Boots smiled, thinking he had always liked calling his friend that, although he went by others like William, Willie and General Hughes. He had helped many soldiers, but the Alliance had not showed any gratitude. Boots reflected on the war and events since. Things would change soon, and he would have a part in seeing that they do.

The speaker on his desk startled him from his thoughts. "Sir, you have another message on that previous frequency."

Boots almost fell out of his chair as he scrambled for the reply button. He thought before speaking. *What the heck is going on out there?* "Send it through."

He impatiently pushed the code on the pad. After a short period it took to decode, the image on the screen made him smile.

The Panthers Return

Tiger's Pride dominated the view outside the viewport Boots had been looking out for the past hour. It had arrived about a day ago, and her robotic commander Mech 1 had cleared up his confused mind. He was expecting company any time, some expected and some not. A flash signaled the arrival of some of his guests. The static-filled voice over the bridge speakers confirmed who it was. Katie spoke to her old friend. "This is *Vixen* requesting permission to land."

Boots could not get the response out quick enough, "Permission to land is granted; your old parking spot is open."

Katie landed in the familiar hangar easier than anywhere else she had landed.

A quartet of friends greeted them when they walked down the ramp. Max was the most excited to see them. He knocked

Jennifer to her knees with his best attempt at a hug. He asked with a static-filled translation, "Can I please go next time?"

She laughed and replied, "We will see."

Mech 1 was right there to help his captain up. "Thanks, big guy."

The three of them joined the others. Katie and Boots were talking. Jennifer noticed that Bethany had held back a little, so she grabbed her hand. "Let's go; I will introduce you. He is a great guy."

Bethany added, "Handsome too, baby."

They just laughed.

Jennifer hugged her friend. "Hi, Boots."

She pulled back to introduce her best friend. "Boots, this is my best friend, Bethany."

He held out his hand; Bethany shook it. Boots looked around and asked where Panther was. Jennifer said, "Getting his stuff I think."

Panther walked down the ramp carrying his gear. Boots went to greet him.

Jennifer had not noticed, but seeing the two together, she realized the two men were wearing the same uniform. She could not hold it in anymore, so she asked Bethany. "You know what is up with that uniform? I have been seeing it a lot lately."

Her friend smiled at her.

Jennifer sighed and grilled her friend some more. "There is that smile again. You know something, don't you?"

Bethany figured now was a good time to say something. "They are Panthers, the elite combat unit from the war. Our traveling companion is a founding member."

Jennifer and Katie said at the same time, "Well, that explains that."

Bethany added, "They disbanded, but many of them stayed in touch."

A ship had moved in sight outside the hangar, and Bethany noticed the markings. "Guys, that's Willie's ship, *Panther II*, isn't it? What is it doing here?"

An alarm sounded, alerting those in the hangar of an incoming ship, and the group moved as the shuttle maneuvered for a landing. A young woman in a white robe ran past them to meet it. She jumped up and down excitedly. They watched her curiously. *Whom was she expecting?*

The door opened, and a helmeted figure stepped out. He was wearing a suit exactly like Panther's, but a darker blue. The young woman hugged him so hard she almost knocked him down. The alarm sounded again.

"More ships coming in, guys; we need to move," Katie said as she motioned for them to move back.

The stranger in the combat suit waved to Boots and Panther and headed toward Katie, Jennifer, and Bethany. He ducked to avoid a landing ship. The sisters became nervous, but Bethany had an idea of who it was. She moved back; if her hunch was right, she wanted to be a safe distance away. Max let out a shallow rumble, and she smiled. The big cat confirmed her hunch.

Sarah held back as well. The man removed his helmet and shock took hold of the sisters.

Katie screamed, "Willie, is it really you?"

The youngest sister leaped into his arms, but Jennifer held back a bit. Then she grabbed him and hugged him just as hard as did her younger sister. Willie looked toward Bethany, and she gestured for him to say nothing about her secret. He nodded his acknowledgment of her wish. He introduced his niece, Sarah, to them, and she excused herself.

Willie sat the two of them down on some nearby crates, because he knew the questions would be flowing like a good wine. Katie started to speak, but he gestured for her to remain quiet. "I am so sorry for the pain you girls have suffered. Let me explain."

He gestured toward Bethany. "After my meeting with Agent Delta, I was on my way back to my shuttle when I ran into an ARES agent, and we got into a fight. Before I could get a shot off, he cut my left arm, causing my monitor to fall off."

He raised his arm to reveal bandages. "That is why the signal went out that I was dead. I got him about the time the alarms sounded, and I found a maintenance hatch. I used a maintenance drone to make my escape, but the explosion threw the drone and me into Jupiter's atmosphere. I spent the next two days or so floating until one of the mining platforms picked up my distress signal. I deliberately kept it on a weak signal so only your dad's mining operation would find me. I am one lucky guy. Thank God, I am here."

Katie spoke and asked, "Why didn't you let anyone know when you got out?"

He smiled at her and continued to explain, "I met with your dad, and he told me what was going on, and we decided to wait until you all we here and safe. If I revealed that I was alive, it may have put you all in danger."

He stood up and hugged them once more. Looking around, he noticed Boots and Panther had joined them. As he turned to speak to them, he remembered something. "Oh, girls, your dad sent this and said he will be here tomorrow."

The three men talked as they walked into the other hangar.

The girls looked at what he had handed them. It was picture of their father and a woman in a wedding dress. They screamed. Bethany looked at the picture. "Guys, I know this woman, she is Charlie and Kenny's mom."

Jennifer said, "You mean the Saturn boys."

Bethany turned the picture over and read aloud, "It says 'Benny and Brenda.'"

The girls walked into the hangar next door. It was full of ships and people. Panther approached them and spoke directly to Bethany. "Commander, your ship, *Sarah Elizabeth*, has arrived."

Jennifer threw her hands in the air. "Well, that explains a lot."

Bethany smiled. "Yes, ladies, I am a Panther like your dad and Willie."

A robot rolled up and handed Bethany a uniform and helmet. As she put on the jump suit and vest, she explained it to them, "My boss asked me to join them about a year ago, saying I would make a great Panther. Willie asked him about me."

She gave them a quick hug and said, "Well, girls, I have to go to work, and we got some payback to dish out. See you in a little bit. Love you."

Bethany hugged Max as she passed him on her way to the shuttle.

The sisters suddenly felt a little left out. Jennifer noticed a gleam in Katie's eye and said, "Oh no, little lady, you are sticking with me."

Katie wondered aloud, "What the heck is going on here?"

Ben and Dylan snuck up behind them, and Ben put his arms around his sisters. "I'll tell you ladies what is going on. It is the return of the Panthers!"

Willie looked at his young friends and gave them a thumbs-up.

Part 3

Rebellion: At War Once More

Attack at Uranus

The rebellion against the Interstellar Alliance, led by the elite combat unit known as Panthers, was only a month old and was growing more intense with the passing of each day. The success of each mission grew more important as well.

Dylan looked up from the computer screen at which he was working and looked around *Saber II*'s small cabin to see what his friends were doing. He looked at his friend Ben sitting on his bunk. He thought to himself how his friend looked odd with the assault rifle in his hand. The two of them had planned to join the military together, but Ben's smarts had presented him with opportunities he could not pass up. Dylan smiled as he stood and headed for the cockpit. A sharp pain streaked up his right leg, causing him to hesitate for an instant. He looked back at Ben, glad his friend had not joined the military. The war had been difficult and had left him with a bad leg. The Alliance surgeons had wanted to replace his leg with a cybernetic one but decided against it due to his persistent protests.

Tyton looked up from the controls as Dylan entered, but did not speak. He simply returned to his work. Sitting in his chair, Dylan looked out the cockpit window at the planet Uranus. Looking around, he noticed the small group of fighters sitting a short distance away on the surface of the moon Cordelia. He thought to himself that the group of fighter pilots had just recently defected from the Interstellar Alliance only a couple weeks earlier. Panther had ordered them to take up a position on this moon, because it was closest to the planet and would provide the best cover.

A loud beeping alarm sounded from the console, pulling him from his thoughts. As Dylan acknowledged and silenced the alarm, a voice crackled over the com speaker. "Hey, guys, that is the mechs coming in."

Ben had heard the alarm and joined them. He spoke. "Is that Jared?"

Dylan answered as he looked out toward the fighter sitting next to them. "Yeah, that is Momma's Boy."

Ben spoke into his headset. "Commander, keep your boys alert. They may attract attention on the way in."

Dylan's younger brother did not respond because he knew to keep silent.

Dylan commented as he watched the transport land between the fighters and *Saber II*, "I wish command had not picked his squad for this mission."

Ben spoke to reassure his friend. "Panther and the others feel his squad is one of the best we have. He will have to be included sooner or later."

Dylan smiled reluctantly in agreement and looked for support from his mechanical friend, Tyton. The robotic marine nodded, and he knew those in command had chosen the right personnel for this mission. He sat back in his chair.

The trio aboard *Saber II* sat in silence for awhile, relieved that the arrival of the mech units earlier had not alerted the nearby Alliance base they were in the system. Dylan had requested mechanical marine units because he trusted few people. An alarm broke the silence, and Ben yelled from the cabin for the others to join him. "Guys, it is time to get it on."

He motioned for Tyton to open the airlock. A figure stepped through, and Ben noticed that it looked similar to Tyton, with only minor differences. Most noticeable was the large combat pack on his back.

The robot, which had been code named Rhino, addressed his superior. "Sir, I was able to get twenty units operational in the time you gave me. The loyalty program we were given was compatible as well."

Dylan replied, impressed at the number available to them, "That is fine, Rhino. I really did not expect that many."

The large robot responded with what seemed to be pride in his voice. "I aim to please, sir."

Ben interrupted with a question that caught Dylan and Tyton by surprise, "Are the cyborg pilots I requested with you?"

Rhino replied, "Yes, sir, and command sent a hacker unit as well."

The others composed themselves and began to protest.

Dylan spoke for both of them. "Why do we need pilots? No one is piloting this bucket but us."

Ben understood where his friends were coming from and quickly attempted to reassure them. "I requested them. They will be better suited to pilot us in."

Tyton moved toward him and Dylan got in between them. Ben nervously explained the plan. "Guys, settle down. We all know that you both are well-capable pilots. I requested cyborg pilots because their reflexes are better than those of a mechanical pilot. Besides I would feel more comfortable with you guys on the ground and we need pilots behind the controls during the mission to insure a speedy escape."

The brief moment of tension subsided as Tyton spoke. "He is correct, sir."

Dylan laughed and said, "Well then, let's get on with it. What you got in mind?"

Rhino motioned for the others to follow as he spoke. "The command tent is set up."

Ben and Dylan put on their helmets and pressurized their suits for the short walk to the temporary lunar structure. They moved along holding to a tether line.

The two cyborg pilots passed as they walked toward the *Saber II*. Dylan grabbed the closest one by the arm. "I'll be right back. Sit and do not touch anything till I get back."

The pilot smiled through his helmet's protective visor. "As you wish sir; it is your ship after all. We will touch nothing."

Dylan walked on, a little annoyed. He could not figure out what annoyed him most. *Was it how polite he was or that he seemed familiar?* He shook his head as he entered the airlock.

Dylan walked over to stand by his younger brother Jared, and they exchanged a quick greeting. Ben activated the data display unit. Their commander, Panther, addressed the small group. "I want to first wish you luck in your mission. Your target is an Alliance facility on the moon known as Portia; it is approximately 16,345 km. from your present location. Our intelligence marks it as a weapons factory. What kind of weapons manufactured there is a mystery to us. The priority of your mission is to take it out, but if possible find out the type of weapons manufactured there. Knowing what type of weapons they are manufacturing will help us calculate future Alliance offensive plans."

Ben made a comment. "That is where the hacker unit comes in."

Panther responded to the younger man's comment, although one was not requested. "Yes, Ben, that is correct, and I want a marine unit assigned to protect it."

Rhino motioned to a nearby mechanical unit, and it responded by moving to stand beside the small tracked robot.

A short time later, the briefing ended, and after final preparations were complete, everyone was in position and ready to go. Jared gave his pilots the order to fire up their engines, and the small fighters hovered to cover the larger transports. Dylan assisted the pilots in the cockpit and left to join the others in the cabin. Dylan had discovered why the pilot seemed familiar before—because he had served with him on a mission during the Mars War. This made him feel a little more comfortable allowing him to pilot his ship. He sat beside his large friend and whispered. "Hey Tyton, I know our pilot. He is good."

Tyton gave him the thumbs-up sign.

Rhino sat across from them, and he asked, "Are you satisfied with the selection of our pilot, sir?"

Dylan put on his helmet and flipped the switch to darken the visor. Just as it began to darken, he flashed Rhino a sly smile.

The transports flew through Uranus' rings, and their pilots made course adjustments that would allow them to fly out and then in toward the moon Portia. The fighters took a straight approach, more suitable for strafing runs. They needed to draw the factory's defensive fire away from the troop transports. As the fighters reached the point of no return, laser turrets filled the sky with energy blasts. The lead fighters fired missiles, and within seconds, explosions rocked the facility.

The *Saber II* swooped in at speed that allowed it to make an assault landing, but also evade fire from laser turrets. Dylan listened closely to the transmissions between the ships and heard the pilot codenamed Condor request that one of the escort fighters take out the door to the hangar that had begun to close. He heard the familiar voice of his brother and gasped as he and Ben looked at one another.

Jared said, "I am on it, Condor."

A few brief seconds later, a missile hit against the door, jamming it open.

"Thanks. That will do, flyboy," the pilot in *Saber II*'s cockpit said just as he was interrupted by a laser blast. The fighters responded with lasers of their own, taking out the hangar's defense cannons. Ben laughed as he watched his friends. He could tell they were itching to be in the cockpit.

He yelled to them. "Easy, guys, we will be on the ground soon."

Dylan acknowledged his comment by gripping his rifle and cocking it. "Oh yeah, it is on, boys!"

The *Saber II* entered the hangar, barely missing the top of the opening with the similar transport flown by Condor close behind. As the other ship sat down on the deck, *Saber II* remained hovering. The gunners on board her showered the landing bay's back wall with laser fire. The landing bay's control station was obliterated, along with the exit in the rear of the bay. Ben was out of *Saber II*'s door before her landing gear touched the deck, and he took a position to cover the others. The others jumped out close behind. Several of the mechanical marines had joined them beside *Saber II*, and Ben was talking to one of them. Dylan could not hear him but knew what he was saying by his gestures. He thought to himself, *He is giving them orders to protect my baby.*

Tyton signaled for him to move, and they headed for the hole in the wall where a door had been earlier. Ben joined them a few seconds later.

Ben turned his fist in the air, and Dylan looked back toward the ships just in time to see them turn in unison to face the hangar door. Dylan looked at his friend, impressed. The battle-hardened marine could not help but notice that his friend had become a natural leader since their trip to Nebula One a few short months ago. Ben's smarts and skills never failed to impress those he met.

The small assault group met unexpectedly low resistance as they made their way to the command center, which made Ben and Dylan a little bit uneasy.

Dylan yelled to the marine unit guarding the hacker robot. "Hey Guardian, tell the little guy to download that data as quick as it can."

The two robots exchanged a short conversation of whistles and static voice, and the larger one gestured to his commanders.

Tyton left his partner Rhino at the door to inform the others of the battle progress. "Guys, the units at the reactor and factory sector are seeing marginal resistance and report most of the combatants appear to be mechanical commandos. Most of the humans must have evacuated when the fighters came in."

Ben and Dylan talked among themselves to assess the situation. "Base schematics show a bay of escape pods on the far side of the moon."

They decided to pull the units from the factory and redirect them to the reactor.

Tyton spoke with his mechanical voice into his headset unit. "Squad two, set explosives on the doors and seal off the factory. Proceed to the reactor. We need to wrap this up before the Alliance reinforcements arrive."

A movement from the shadows caught Ben's and Dylan's attention. However, Tyton was distracted by the transmissions in his headset and took a blast in the back, falling against a nearby console. Ben took a shot, and the lone figure fell down into the operations pit with a thud.

Dylan was first to reach Tyton, and his mechanical friend relayed the message that had just came over his headset. "Sir, the squad at the reactor has accomplished its mission, and they say it will go critical in a short time. They are already on the way back to the ships. You need to leave me, because I cannot move."

Ben told Dylan, "Hey, man, we got to get out of here."

Ben looked toward the little robot at the console and yelled. "Hacker, you need to disconnect from the terminal and head for the ship."

The little robot did not need to be told twice as it rolled for the door as fast as it could move with its guardian close behind.

Ben turned to his friend. "We got to go!"

Dylan became irate. "I am not leaving anyone behind!"

Tyton urged his friend to go. "Sir, I am no different than the other units we have lost here. You need to leave me."

Dylan whispered, "Yes, you are; you are my friend."

Ben turned away from his friends to answer a message coming in from the fighters outside. "Commander, our sensors show the reactor is about to explode. Why are you guys still in there?"

Ben responded to Jared's call. "We have run into some trouble."

The response Ben got did not surprise him. "We got trouble out here too; Alliance ships have entered the system."

Ben gave the other ship the order to take off as he turned to his friends. "Hostile ships in the system; we need to go!"

Dylan yelled. "I am not leaving Tyton behind!"

The remaining marine unit known as Rhino walked over to them, removed his pack, and picked up Tyton effortlessly as he spoke. "Leaving him is not an issue, sir; let's get out of here."

When they arrived at the hangar, the rear ramp of the *Saber II* was already lowered, and they ran onboard with the remaining marine units following behind.

Just as they left, the hangar explosions tore the facility apart.

They joined the remaining ships a short distance from the moon and began their escape. Shortly before reaching a safe distance to make a jump into light speed, the other transport exploded as blasts from several of the pursuing ships ripped through it.

The exploding ship startled Ben, and he looked out as the last of the blast disappeared. He yelled to the others, "We lost transport two." Just as the words were out of his mouth, the *Saber II* rocked as a blast grazed her hull, but the ship made the jump to light speed and safety, followed closely by the remaining fighters. The attack at Uranus was a success but not without a cost.

Ladies Called to Action

Katie sat on the deck in the weapons training facility, onboard her sister's ship *Tiger's Pride*. The tears in her eyes were due more to frustration than the pain in her left shoulder. As she looked down at the assault rifle sitting beside her, she thought aloud. "I am not going to let you get the best of me."

Jennifer spoke from the door, where she had been watching her little sister. "Talking to guns now, sis?"

Katie jumped up, grabbing the assault rifle as she stood. She walked over to join Jennifer, who had sat on a nearby bench. "Jen, this is the only weapon we got that I cannot qualify with."

Jennifer took the rifle and attempted to comfort her. "Katie, you do not have to know how to use every weapon we have; besides, you are an expert on all the others. In fact, you are better than Ben on a lot of them. If you tell him I said that, I'll deny it."

Katie laughed and rubbed her shoulder. "Okay, but one day I am going to qualify on this thing." Katie took the rifle from her sister as she headed for the door.

"Hey, let's get something to drink. You've been in there every day for about a month, and you need a break," Jennifer said as she punched Katie on the shoulder playfully, as they strolled down the hall.

Katie jerked back and gave a serious look toward her older sister. "Well, I want to be ready when I am needed."

Jennifer smiled at Katie as she looked back from the elevator door. "It may be sooner than you may think. I got a call from Dad, and he said Panther wants to see us."

Katie leaped into the elevator excitedly. "What do you think he wants?"

Her older sister said nothing, only smiled. The door shut behind them.

After a short break and a quick shower, Katie joined her sister in the ship's docking bay. As she walked in, Max ran to meet her. He seemed a bit excited to Katie. "I get to come with you this time." He spoke in his familiar, static-filled translated voice.

Katie, curious by his comment, asked. "What is going on, Max?"

As he ran ahead of her to join Jennifer, he replied, "Jennifer will tell you."

Jennifer was busy opening a door to one of the bay's many storage docks.

The metal door rattled as it moved along its tracks, and the dock's lights flickered on to reveal a ship with a tiger on the side. As the deck robot rolled the ship out, Jennifer turned and said, "This is my baby. I call her *Lady Tiger*. We found her onboard when we were cleaning *Tiger's Pride*, and I fixed her up."

Katie recognized the ship's design as an old Mars marine's assault corvette.

"We will be taking her to meet with Dad and Panther."

Katie looked down, a little sad. "We are not taking *Vixen*?"

Jennifer walked over and put her arm around her sister. "Hey, we already used her twice; it is my turn to use my ship. Besides, I have not had her out yet. She needs a shakedown trip."

Katie replied as she rubbed Max's head, who had nudged up against her to comfort her. "I'll be okay, big guy. It is cool, sis. When do we leave?"

Jennifer said, "As soon I get her ready. Go get your stuff. Oh, and, sis, bring some of those guns you are so good with."

Katie ran to get her stuff. She yelled for their tiger companion to join her, "Hey, Max, come on. Give me a little help."

The tiger ran after her, excited to be going along.

A short time later, Katie and Max returned with Katie's things. Mech 1 had joined Jennifer and was helping her load supplies. She spoke as she walked up the ship's ramp. "Sis, where do I put this stuff?"

Jennifer pointed to a row of lockers. "Find a locker; any of those will do."

She turned back to the operations console to power up *Lady Tiger*'s systems.

Katie stood at the top of the ramp waiting for her sister who was talking to her mechanical officer Mech 1. She could not hear what was being said. A short time later, Mech 1 turned to leave and waved to her. She returned the wave good-bye as Jennifer joined her. Her older sister nudged her as she hit the switch to the ramp. "Are you ready to go?"

Katie smiled and said, "Oh yeah, can I fly the ship?"

They laughed as they climbed the stairs to the cockpit.

Katie looked at an empty seat just behind and above Jennifer. "Do I sit there?"

Jennifer looked up from the pilot's console and smacked the seat beside her. "No, little lady, you are my copilot. That is the navigator's station up there."

Lady Tiger's hovering thrusters ignited, moving her across the deck toward the hangar bay door. Jennifer saw Mech 1 watching just out of the way and saluted to him. He returned the salute as the ship dropped down and out of the hangar.

As they flew away from *Tiger's Pride*, Katie asked. "By the way, sis, where are we going?"

Jennifer smiled at her. "You are asking now. We are heading for a position near Saturn. Bethany is supposed to be there too. The ship jumped to light speed on its way to Saturn."

A short time later, an alarm sounded, and Max jumped from a nap. Jennifer and Katie ran into the cockpit. Max asked, "What's up? Are we there?"

Katie pulled his tail playfully as she sat at the copilot's seat. Max stood up from his napping spot behind Katie's chair and put his paws on the center console. He was careful not to hit any controls. He looked out the window at the planet Saturn in the distance. Jennifer jumped up to the navigator's seat and entered a course change. As the ship turned to starboard, Katie noticed a blip on the console. "There they are. We will be there in a few minutes."

A few short minutes later, *Lady Tiger* arrived at their destination. The blip that showed as one ship was in fact two ships. The ships were docked to a mobile docking cross, which was designed to allow ships to dock together in remote locations. Jennifer maneuvered the ship to the airlock across from Bethany's ship, *Kit-Cat*. With a clang, the ship was docked. In a brief moment, the trio exited the airlock into the round center chamber and was greeted by a pair of Panther marines. One directed them to the airlock to their left, which led into the waiting marine medium attack cruiser.

Bethany greeted them and gestured for them to sit at a nearby table. Katie curiously asked, "Bethany, why are you being so cold?"

Bethany smiled and touched Katie's hand. "Sorry, Katie, I just got my game face on."

Bethany stood as Panther entered from the cockpit. "Hello, girls, your dad will be in shortly. He is working on the data for your mission. He wanted to do it personally."

Bethany asked as she sat down, "Sir, I have known about this mission for a few days. Where will we be going?"

Panther looked at the small group an instant before speaking. "Your target is in the Neptune system on the moon Triton."

Benny stepped into the room from the control room, and Katie jumped up to hug him. He returned her hug and took a chair in between his daughters and passed out data display pads. "Katie, Jennifer, and Bethany, this is your mission data. Your target is a communications station on the moon Triton. Neptune has crossed Pluto's orbit and for a few years will be the farthest from the sun, making the station vital to Interstellar Alliance communications with outer colony stations."

Panther spoke up from the side of the room. "We have supplied you with the data you need. How you carry out your mission is up to you three."

The trio of young women looked surprised at each other.

A short time later, the meeting ended and Katie and Jennifer visited briefly with their father.

Bethany met them in the center chamber, and Jennifer overheard Bethany talking to her aide, so she held back a moment. "Take *Kit-Cat* back to the *Sarah Elizabeth*."

The young officer turned and left to carry out her orders.

Jennifer nudged her friend and said, "Are you ready to go?"

Bethany picked up her pack and said, "Yes, we need to go soon; we are risking detection the longer we stay here."

As they turned to join Katie, the sound of *Kit-Cat* detaching from the clamps startled Jennifer.

Soon the trio aboard *Lady Tiger* was on their way.

Katie looked out the window from the navigation station. She saw her father looking at them and waved as the larger ship clamped onto the mobile dock and flew away.

Bethany helped Katie as she worked on setting course for Neptune, and shortly she sat in the copilot's seat. "The course is set, Jennifer. We can go anytime you are ready."

Without saying a word, Jennifer positioned her ship for the light speed jump. Max laid down behind Bethany.

A moment later, they leaped into light speed and into the awaiting adventure.

Ladies' Night Out

Jennifer and the others had arrived at Neptune a few days earlier and decided a covert operation was best. The night before Bethany and Jennifer had carried out a recon survey of the moon, and the time to get their mission done had finally come.

The group had split into two pairs, and Max had joined his friend Jennifer in her tasks. He stood looking around the lunar surface, watching for anything that might put their mission in jeopardy. His keen eyesight was a definite benefit as a lookout. Although he wore his S.E.P.A. suit Jennifer had promised him, he still was nervous. "See anything out there, Max?" Jennifer's voice cracked in his modified communications headset unit. The nervous tiger looked in his friend's direction, where she worked at planting explosives and shook his head to signal his answer.

A moment later, his answer changed, because his keen sight detected a patrol craft approaching. "Hey, a ship is coming."

Jennifer motioned for him to take cover and relayed the message to the others.

Katie and Bethany scampered for cover behind a nearby power transfer station. Katie grabbed her assault rifle and took aim for a shot. Bethany put her hand nervously on Katie's shoulder. "We need to do this quietly, little lady." Katie flashed a reassuring smile and turned to watch the ship approach. She watched nervously as it passed over Jen and Max's position and then theirs. The patrol passed without noticing them. Bethany continued her work, and Katie returned to her lookout position. Bethany smiled as she looked at her young friend and thought of how she had argued against a covert operation. She had wanted a more direct assault. She understood why Katie felt that and admired her courage.

The remainder of the lunar faze of their operation went without incident, and they returned to the hotel suite that they had acquired as part of the cover they had planned. The girls were tired and went to sleep almost immediately. Max sat near Jennifer's bed still anxious from their trip out on the surface. Jennifer said as she got into her bed, "You did well today, Max. Try to get some sleep, Max. Good night." The tiger responded with a low growl. Several sleepless hours passed for him. The restless tiger got up and left the room after a quick glance to see if Jennifer was okay. He walked around the suite. He checked in on Katie first then Bethany. He noticed Bethany was not in her bed, so he proceeded to look for her and found her in the suite's kitchenette. She patted his head as she passed him, and he followed her to the couch.

Max broke the silence, with the static voice from his translation device. "Are you okay?"

Bethany answered her curious tiger friend, "I am okay, just thinking about things."

He did not ask her what she was thinking about; he only sat quietly beside her. Bethany sipped her milk and spoke, "Max, our friends are great."

She looked toward the bedrooms, and the tiger looked in that direction as well. As she spoke, he turned his attention to her once more. "Jen and Katie have really impressed me on this mission. I know this is not our first mission together, but this one is different. On the last one, we had the guys along, but we are on our own here."

Max sensed something was bothering her and put his head on her lap.

Jennifer woke up, heard her friend's voice in the other room, and wondered to whom she was talking. She got out of bed to investigate and paused at the door when she saw what was beyond it. She watched as her two best friends sat on the couch. It was the first time the two had ever gotten close, so she did not want to disturb them.

Bethany continued, not aware that Jennifer was behind her.

"Jen and Katie have been affected more by those jerks in the Interstellar Alliance. More than I have. They have been through a lot these last few years with the loss of their mom and grandmother. They have handled themselves like professionals on this mission; I am trained for stuff like this, but they have picked up things quickly. Max, I am glad they are here with me."

He rumbled a response, and Bethany laughed. Jennifer wiped her eyes and walked back to her bed. As a tear fell on the pillow, she thought to herself, *Bethany is a good friend; I hope I do not let her down.* A short time later, Jennifer fell back to sleep because she was still a bit tired.

The girls slept late the following morning because the final phase of the mission would be completed late in the evening.

Later that evening, the girls went dancing at the bar near their hotel. They danced to some music from the late twentieth century. Katie had recognized it was from the 1980s, because vintage music was a hobby of hers. Max sat just outside the open doorway that lead to the courtyard between the bar and hotel. The bartender would not allow him to enter despite Jennifer's protest. Jennifer and Max had been there before while on a business trip for Falcon Intergalactic and some of the regulars remembered him. Jennifer became a little embarrassed when the bartender reminded her of what had happened. Her tiger friend had spilled a pitcher of beer on a server and scared quite a few patrons while attempting to protect her from some jerk who had been bothering her.

The three young women had fun dancing and flirting with the pilots and local guys. They were not interested in getting to know any of them because they would be gone soon. Max watched faithfully as a few patrons nervously walked by. He paid little attention to those not close to the girls. Several hours passed without anything happening, but Bethany and Jennifer had decided to turn up the heat and complete their mission. Bethany approached a drunken freighter pilot and whispered something to him, and he staggered over to where Jennifer and Katie were sitting. Bethany lifted her glass to signal her friends, and Max became a bit more alert.

The pilot, inspired by Jennifer's looks and nudged on by the booze in his belly, began his attempt to seduce her. She played along a little while to make things a bit tenser and draw a little attention to ensure an alibi. After a few minutes, Bethany joined them and needed to reassure Katie of the plan, because the man was saying things that bothered her. She whispered into Katie's ear, "Hey, Katie, it will be over soon. Jen knows how to handle that guy."

Although Bethany was close to her, she barely heard her. They watched the guy and Jennifer talking. He said something that made Katie's blood boil, and she reached for a gun in one of her boots. Things became seriously tense, Max stood, and Jennifer gestured toward him to stay out of it. The angry tiger reluctantly held back. Bethany looked at her friend and realized it was time to end things. Just as the bouncer and bartender approached, Bethany punched a code on her arm communication unit. After a brief moment, a distant explosion rocked through the small spaceport.

The atmosphere began to escape from the surrounding corridors, knocking the drunken patrons and other residents down and pulling anything not secured toward the direction where the breach in the structure was. Within several seconds, a security blast door slammed in the distance, sealing off the air loss.

A voice blared over a nearby speaker. "All citizens please evacuate the spaceport. An explosion at our power facility has left the port without power, and we are on reserve power only."

A security guard nearby said above the crowd, "You heard them, people; proceed orderly to the escape pods and hangars immediately."

Jennifer helped Katie off the floor and motioned for Bethany and Max to follow. As they walked to the hangar where the *Lady Tiger* waited, she said, "That is our exit call, ladies."

She noticed their pilot friend was almost knocked down by a maintenance robot as it streaked past, heading for the damaged sector. She looked back to see if he was okay and thought, *He was not that bad.*

Bethany noticed her friend's guilt and comforted her. "Sorry he was a pawn in the game. I do not like it either, but I deal with it."

Katie interrupted them. "Hey we need to get out of here."

They hurried toward the hangar unnoticed because everyone else was hurrying too.

Several minutes later, they were onboard the ship, and its engines roared, sounding like a tiger as it swooped out of the hangar door. As they flew away from the spaceport,

Katie commented, "I thought we were supposed to hit the communications station?"

"We did, but not the transmission array."

Bethany smiled at Jennifer, and she turned the ship a little to the starboard. Bethany tapped her communication unit and gestured for Katie to look toward Neptune. A structure in orbit above the planet's North Pole was destroyed in a massive explosion. Katie looked back surprised, and before she could say anything, Bethany said, "I'll tell how we did it another time."

The ship entered light speed safely. Katie sighed from the navigator's seat. "What a girls' night out."

Something to Prove (Daddy's Girl Goes It Alone)

Katie sat in *Big Rock*'s astronomy dome, where she spent most of her free time. Boots had offered her command of the station when the girls returned from Neptune a short three months ago. Her thoughts were far too serious for a woman of her age, but the events of the rebellion weighed heavily on her mind. Although she loved being in command of *Big Rock*, she still thought she could do more.

She looked out at the stars in the direction in which her sister, Jennifer, had gone.

The door opened and a small robot rolled in, followed by her father, Benny. "Hey, this little guy has been looking for you."

She patted the little robot as he stopped by her side. "Hi, Shorty, where have you been?"

Her father laughed and said, "Boots just looked at him and thinks he must have a programming glitch because he has never seen a robot take up with a human like this."

She answered him with a grin, "Yeah, we call it the puppy dog glitch. He has been by my side since we got here from Neptune."

Katie looked away from her father, noticeably frustrated, and he asked her what was wrong. She walked over to a nearby console and sat down. She looked back at him and began to explain, "Dad, I want to be doing more to help out."

Her father sat silently listening.

"I love being commander of this station, but I feel I should be doing more. You think Panther has a mission I could carry out?"

Benny hesitated, and Katie prodded him with her finger. He took her hand and said, "You are my little girl."

He caught himself and realized what he was doing. He knew Katie could take care of herself and do anything she put her mind to. He smiled and pulled her toward the door. "Come on; let's go see him. He has just arrived."

They left the room, shut the door, and suddenly realized their little companion was still inside. Katie opened the door and little, blue robot rolled out whistling erratically.

"Sorry about that, Shorty."

The trio walked down the hall heading for the command deck.

Early the next morning Katie prepared for her mission. The hangar was quiet because most on the station's crew had not awakened from their sleep yet. Boots entered the hangar, just getting off the graveyard shift on the command deck, to say good-bye to his friend. "Good morning, little lady. Why are you in a hurry?"

Katie looked up at him from her work at fueling *Vixen* and handed the fuel hose to the hangar's maintenance robot. The robot moved away, not paying much attention to the two humans, who stood silently for a short time. Both found it difficult to say good-bye. Shorty rolled down the rear ramp, whistling as if trying to whistle some tune, breaking the tension and causing them to laugh. Boots spoke first, "That little guy has been like that since he returned from the attack on the Uranus factory."

Katie continued her work as she spoke. "I like him that way; it gives him personality."

Katie's father ran into the hangar with his shirt unbuttoned. In his rush to see his little girl off, he had not bothered to worry about how he looked. He shot Boots a quick greeting and hugged Katie tightly. "I am glad I caught you. Why didn't you wake me?"

Katie spoke softly, "I did not want to disturb you; I thought you could use the sleep. You really seemed tired last night."

Benny spoke with a crackle in his voice, "I am never too tired to say good-bye."

Katie sensed her father's sadness and spoke to reassure him, "Dad, I will be okay. I can take care of myself."

He smiled at her because he knew she was right. She returned a smile and said, "Dad, I got to go."

She hugged him and said bye to Boots. She walked up the ramp and stopped to wave one more time as her little sidekick rolled by her. She hit a button on the wall, closing the ramp.

The two men moved away as Katie moved her ship, *Vixen*, into position for takeoff. Benny noticed how his daughter maneuvered the ship around the crowded hangar and felt a little bit better about her going out by herself. *Vixen* left the hangar, leaving silence in her wake. Boots broke the silence to reassure his companion. "Hey, she will be okay. I talked to her last night, and she agreed to meet one of our contacts on Mars when she gets there."

Benny felt better as the two of them left the hangar. "Want a cup of coffee? You look like you could use one."

Katie landed on Mars's moon, Phobos, late in the evening ready to get her mission started. She spoke to Shorty, "Well, little guy, we are here."

She laughed because the robot responded in a way that seemed like fear. "Don't worry; I will take care of you. Besides, I need you. Your hacker skills will be helpful on our mission. Having you as a companion got me this mission."

Early the next morning, Katie sat in a small spaceport café waiting for the person that Panther said would meet her. She had finished one cup of coffee and had ordered another before anyone else came in. She had started to think she had been forgotten, when a tall, slender woman about her age entered the café and approached her.

The stranger introduced herself, "Hello, my name is Jade. Panther tells me you are needing access to the Alliances Intelligence facility."

Katie nodded her agreement, wanting to say as little as possible. The two women talked a short time, mostly small talk to make sure no one suspected anything. Jade stood first and motioned for Katie to follow, and as they left the café, she explained what they would need to do. "Come on; my ship is this way."

Katie seemed a bit puzzled because she thought she would be taking *Vixen* to the surface. A strange feeling began to grow in her stomach. She looked back to make sure Shorty was with them and followed Jade.

A quick shuttle ride and a short walk, Katie made it to her destination. She read the sign on the door, and it said Interstellar Alliance Intelligence Headquarters. The place was deserted because it was still a bit early. She heard a frantic whistle from Shorty and turned to see what was up, only to find a gun pointed at her.

"What is going on?"

Before Jade could speak, a sound of gun blast came from behind her, and she fell into Katie's arms. Katie looked quickly at the dead woman she held in her arms and then in the direction the blast had come from. Confusion and shock both rushed through her mind. A tall, dark-haired young man stood before her holding a laser pistol in his hand. Katie spoke first. "Aaron Jackson Robinson, what is going on? Why did you kill Jade?"

He smiled and said, "Hi, cutie. You used to call me A. J."

Katie responded. "That was a long time ago."

She shook her head to shake away the rush of emotions. "I said, 'What is going on?'"

His face turned serious. "Well, she was going to kill you. Katie, the alliance knows that you and your family are part of the rebellion. They suspected Panther would send agents on missions here. Jade was sent to intercept you."

Katie laid the dead woman on the ground and sat on a nearby bench. A. J. sat beside her and spoke again. "I did not know it was you she would be meeting."

Katie stood, not sure if she could trust her old friend. "You knew I was coming?"

He shook his head. "I worked with Jade; she was a great agent back before she got into some trouble. She knew about the corruption in the alliance government, but her love and need for money influenced her. I followed her because I knew she had orders to kill any rebel agents. Then she met you." He began to explain that Jade had killed her real contact.

He paused a moment. "I could not allow her to kill you because you are my friend despite what happened in the past. Listen to me, Katie. I do not like what is going on here, but I have to live here. At least till things change."

He stood and motioned for her to follow. "I will help you get back to your ship."

Katie stood and protested, "Hey! I came here to complete a mission, and I am going to do that because I am trying to change things."

He looked back at her, and after a short stare from her, he agreed to help her complete her mission. He and Katie quickly moved Jade's body and cleaned up where she had been lying.

Due to the events earlier in the day, Katie had to postpone her mission until late in the night. She and her robot companion waited in the shadows near their target for her old friend A. J. Seeing him again brought back the memory of the last time she had seen him. She remembered how difficult it had been ending their school-time romance, but she realized it was the right thing to do. They were growing apart, and Katie's career was starting at a dizzying pace. She did not have time for a boyfriend back then. She smiled as she thought, *Not much time for a guy these days either*.

She was brought back to the present by the sounds of someone leaving the Intelligence Headquarters. Shorty let out a faint whistle, and Katie whispered to herself, "Yeah, Shorty, that is the last of them. A. J. should be here soon."

A short time later, the small robot received a signal and touched Katie with a mechanical claw to get her attention. She turned and saw her friend motion for her to follow him to the back entrance.

He spoke quietly, "I have the code to the door for you."

Before he finished speaking, the little robot had the alarm deactivated and the door opened.

Katie smiled at her surprised friend. "What can I say? He is good. It must be the upgrades he recently had done."

They had to hurry to keep up with the little robot and caught up as he found the data terminal he was looking for.

She spoke to Shorty as if scolding him. "Hey! Short stuff, this is our mission. You mind letting me help?"

Katie took up a position to keep a look out for any company and saw A. J. laughing. "What you laughing at?"

He said nothing, only shook his head.

A short time later, the robot finished the data retrieval and joined Katie by the door. He showed her a file he tagged as important.

As A. J. joined them, Shorty retracted the small view screen back into his body. Katie spoke, "We need to get this back to my commanders quick, so I need to get back up to Phobos and my ship."

The young man gestured for them to follow. "I have a hover scout nearby, and my ship is a short ride in the mountains to the east."

A short time later, Katie stood beside *Vixen*, saying good-bye once again to a friend she cared a lot about. Her career was once again whisking her away. "Well, I guess we need to get going; that data Shorty is carrying is real important to us."

She hugged A. J. and quickly ran up the ramp. She hesitated at the top and looked back. She asked A. J. a simple question, "Why don't you come with us?"

A. J. smiled. "I belong here. I will do what I can here without getting into trouble."

Katie waved as the ramp closed. "I had to ask. Bye."

The young man Katie called A. J. watched as she moved her ship toward the hangar door. He thought to himself, *I wish I was going with her, but I would only slow her down. I will miss you.*

Katie flew around Mars, and she set the coordinates for her trip home. She was gone with a flip of a switch.

A Desperate Battle (Friends Fall)

The space station called *Big Rock* drifted in the outer rim near the dwarf planet Pluto.

A month had passed since Katie had returned from Mars, and the others had joined her on *Big Rock*. Katie stood looking out the command deck's main viewport at the trio of large ships just beyond.

Bethany had returned in the Saturn-class battleship named *Sarah Elizabeth*. She had assumed command of the massive warship at the start of the rebellion. Her friend Boots had arrived just last night in a Saturn-class destroyer he had named *Lone Star*.

She looked at the third large ship and could not help but smile because it had a special place in her heart. *Tiger's Pride* had been a source of many fond memories for her.

The silence of the early morning ended with the crackling voice of her father through her headset communicator. "This is Commander Graham; my group is ready to leave."

Katie did not respond. She allowed the communications officer do so. She looked out toward the main docking tower as her father's medium attack cruiser, *Spirit of Oma*, disconnected. It was joined by two others.

Another familiar voice came through her headset; it was Tyton. "This is unit two. We are ready for light speed."

The radio chatter continued until the ships went into light speed.

The man Katie knew as Uncle Willie joined her and spoke to her. "Your dad will be okay; his soldiers and mech units are some of the best we have. Tyton said he would be by his side during the campaign on Mars."

Willie gestured for her to join him in a cup of coffee, and they discussed station affairs. The morning passed quietly into afternoon. Incoming reports from the capital ships were the only exciting events.

The quietness that filled the morning was shattered early in the afternoon as alarms blared and sensor screens filled with a small fleet of Alliance warships and fighters.

Max put his paws against the *Tiger's Pride* viewport and looked at the approaching ships. "We are under attack!"

He immediately was at Jennifer's side because he most definitely did not want to get in the way.

If this had happened to him seven or eight months earlier, he would have been frantic. But he, as well as the others, had become battle hardened.

Almost immediately, a pair of enemy fighters hit the station. Their target was the solar collectors and the generator cooling station.

Without being asked, Jennifer moved *Tiger's Pride* in a defensive position as Boots and Bethany's ships engaged the enemy capital ships.

Katie looked at the sensor on her chair, as the *Saber II* entered the battle, and worry filled her heart for the second time today. She realized that the worry was only going to get greater, and it did as a group of fighters launched from the maintenance deck. Her cousin Jared flew the lead fighter. All of the gang was in the middle of it now.

She felt a little relieved as Panther flew up alongside Ben and Dylan in his ship *X*-13. Katie listened close as his voice crackled from the speaker. "Are you two ready to play?"

Ben responded in a confident voice, "Yeah let's do this."

Jared jumped into the radio chatter, "Hey don't leave me out."

Dylan answered his younger brother, "Well, hello, Momma's Boy. Glad you could join us."

Katie smiled as she listened because when the guys worked as a team like this, the enemy lost many fighters. She remembered the first time they did so; it was in a battle near the asteroid belt. It worked well then, and she prayed it would now.

The battle, now about thirty minutes old, was fast becoming intense.

Bethany's ship, the *Sarah Elizabeth*, was well armed and holding its own against a Mars-class cruiser. Boots' *Lone Star* was in a bit harder fight, but it was holding on as one of the cruisers it was engaging lost power and drifted away from the confrontation.

Panther, Ben, Dylan, and Jared with his wingman continued to take on the Alliance fighters, having some success. Jennifer, aboard *Tiger's Pride*, yelled orders as the ship attempted to defend *Big Rock*, which was throwing a few punches of her own. Katie watched the floating enemy cruiser as the other two moved away, still fighting. When she felt it was far enough away from *Lone Star*, she gave an order for a missile assault on it. The explosions ripped the enemy ship apart across its hull.

An alarm sounded, and Katie and William went to check long-range sensors and did not like what they saw. Katie spoke franticly. "William, we cannot defend against that many ships. We have been fighting for almost an hour." He saw the panic in her face. He grabbed her by the arm and led her into the hallway.

"Katie, I need you to listen to me. You know what I know about the Alliance. I will not lie to you. We are in a desperate battle. I want you, your sibling, and friends to get out of here." Katie protested, but William stopped her. "Katie, I am not asking you to run; I need to go on a mission. I am giving you the Omega code. Do you know what I mean?"

Tears filled Katie's eyes, and she hugged her best friend tightly. He pulled away from his youngest friend. "Go now. We don't have much time!"

Katie screamed for her little robotic friend as she ran for the elevators. "Shorty, come on! We need to go!" The little robot hurried to her side. She saluted her friend as the elevator door shut.

A minute later aboard *Saber II* an alarm sounded as it did on all the other ships. Dylan shouted, "Dang, Willie just sent out the Omega code."

The two glanced at each other. They all knew what that code meant and what they needed to do. Jennifer began to cry as she looked toward the *Big Rock*'s hangars.

She heard Katie's voice over the speakers. "*Tiger's Pride,* I have been ordered to join you. I will be there shortly."

She thought aloud. "Come on, Katie. Get over here."

Mech 1 walked up beside her and said in his mechanical voice, "We are being ordered to move away from the station."

"Do it!" Jennifer shouted to the helm officer, and he immediately carried out her order. As *Tiger's Pride* moved away, Boots ordered his ship to move in to defend the station under the cover of missile fire from *Big Rock*.

Katie safely landed aboard *Tiger's Pride* after eluding an enemy fighter and hurried to the bridge. As she reached the bridge, Jennifer met her. "Bethany made it out, and she is on her way to earth."

Jennifer saw pain on her sister's face, a pain she had not seen since her mom's death. "Why did Willie give the Omega code?"

Katie wiped tears from her eyes. "A large Alliance attack fleet is on its way here. We picked it up on long-range sensors. I have orders here to head for Nebula One. There is no time to explain." She spoke to Shorty, and he rolled to a console and quickly entered the coordinates. The helm responded and the ship began to move out of the battle zone.

A blast close to Jared blinded him for a moment, allowing an enemy fighter to score a direct hit on his engines. His fighter's escape system engaged, throwing his cockpit away from the explosion. Panther quickly responded and set down cover fire, as Dylan piloted *Saber II* into position to retrieve his little brother. Panther gave Dylan the order to make his emergency light speed jump. He hesitated, and Panther yelled from the speaker. "Go now, that is an order."

A moment before the *Saber II* went into light speed, Ben saw Panther flying toward *Big Rock* to help his friends.

Tiger's Pride neared its jump point, slowed by a small swarm of enemy fighters. Katie and Jennifer watched from the rear bridge, and Katie still protested. "I do not want to leave them."

The instant she finished the sentence, three robotic alliance cruisers jumped from light speed virtually right on top of the *Big Rock*, instantly opening fire.

Katie cried, "Let's go back and help them!"

Seconds before *Tiger's Pride* made its light speed jump, the *Big Rock* exploded in the distance, taking with it the destroyer *Lone Star*.

Katie and Jennifer screamed, "Willie!" as *Tiger's Pride* jumped into light speed.

Part 4

Reasons to Continue the Fight

The Reunion

Katie looked out the viewport at a large ship floating nearby. She thought about how the ship they called *Big Willie* had become a constant companion to the rebellion's new command station *MS*-1023. Although similar to *Big Rock,* this station had no drive engines of its own, so it depended on the large barge to move it around space.

Katie looked closely at the name on the ship's hull, and tears began to fill her eyes. It had been a month since she lost her friends William and Boots in the tragic explosion near Pluto. She swallowed deep in an attempt stop the rush of emotion, as she thought to herself, *I cannot afford to get emotional now; we have too much to do.*

She turned and looked around the room at the group gathered for the briefing. As she watched them, she began to mentally note who was there and who was not.

The ones that came to mind instantly were her father, Boots, and her long-time friend William. She remembered the last time she had seen the man she called Willie. He had sent her and her sister, Jennifer, on a mission to the planet Nebula One. She had reluctantly left her friend behind. She now realized that he had made the right choice and did what needed to be done. She thought how their friend Boots had stood valiantly by his side in his ship *Lone Star*, when the Alliance's robotic cruisers had jumped the station.

Her thoughts drifted to her father, and she whispered to herself. "Dad, I miss you so much."

Her father's campaign on Mars had met unexpected resistance and failed, resulting in his capture. Although several attempts were made to locate him, the small group of rebels was unsuccessful. The leaders in the Alliance had declared martial law on the planet and strengthened the planetary defenses.

She took a seat at a nearby table as she looked at Dylan. He seemed to be lost without his sidekick Tyton. The robotic marine had been retrieved on their first rescue mission, but the technicians were having trouble rebooting his personality program. The marine unit they called Rhino reported that Tyton had taken several hits attempting to get to her father. His last order was for a retreat, one which Tyton was unable to carry out.

She saw a few new faces as well. The most noticeable being the Sasquatch orphans, a male her brother Ben called Big Buford and his sister who had taken the human name Sasha. They had joined the conflict when their parents were killed in an incident with mercenaries during the Interstellar Alliance's attack on their home planet. The leader of Nebula One, although reluctant to join the fight, had agreed to allow the orphans to assist Katie and her siblings in rescuing their father.

Katie smiled as she caught a glimpse of her big brother near the front of the room. He worked with a technical unit, checking some data. Seeing the familiar robot caused her thoughts to drift back to *Big Rock*. Boots' assistant, TU-413, had been lost with the others in the explosion that had destroyed the station.

Ben glanced up and saw his youngest sister looking his way. He shot her a quick smile. Pride swelled in her heart. Katie was so proud of how Ben had embraced the role of leader, after the loss the elder members of the group. He pulled both her and Jennifer up in command roles as well. She was glad she and her sister had not disappointed him.

Jennifer, her thoughts drifted to her big sister. Katie missed her, although she had only been gone a few days. Ben had ordered Jennifer to get *Tiger's Pride* repaired and have its weapons upgraded. The two had spoken earlier, and Jennifer said she would be leaving Mech 1 at the space dock at Neptune, which was now controlled by the rebellion, to oversee the work on the ship and that their cousin Breanna was picking her up on her way to the meeting.

She sighed silently. Bethany had run into some trouble while on her second trip to Earth and was detained by the Earth's government. Ben sent William's nephew Lee and niece Sarah to deal with the negotiations. He also sent Breanna along to retrieve the warship they called *Sarah Elizabeth*, with orders to assume command of it. Katie knew as well as the others that Bethany was a bit hot headed at times, but her skills and talents were assets to the rebellion. She hoped William's family could get her out of trouble quickly and convince Earth to help them. She smiled and thought, *I hope Willie's family can.* She always had loved calling her departed friend Willie.

A sound from the door caught her attention. Her two most amazing and faithful friends entered. The majestic cybernetic tiger called Max and her short, stubby robotic friend, Shorty, approached her. She chuckled at the sight of them. Max seemed proud of his new backpack harness-mounted laser gun. He had said he was glad to have it because he could be more help to Jennifer and the others. This was true, and he had proven that fact a few times since the Sasquatch had presented the idea to Ben. Her little blue friend Shorty had become surprisingly skillful in computer operations and starship navigation. The robotic technicians had studied him several times so they could upgrade the other robotic units. The two of them joined her, and she greeted them. "Hi, guys."

Max spoke in his familiar static voice. "The doc robot says Panther is improving but cannot give a time when he can be revived. They are continuing to administer subliminal data updates to him, so when he is revived he will know what is going on."

Katie patted the tiger on the head and thanked him for the message. The tiger spoke again. "Oh, I almost forgot, they want to know if a real-time feed will be needed during today's meeting to him."

Katie answered him quietly, "I'll call them about that before we get started."

Emotions welled up once more, and she stood and went to the viewport to compose herself. Her friend known to all of them as Panther had been injured in an attempt to help Willie and Boots. Ben and Dylan had rescued him shortly after the battle. His ship, X-13, had sustained severe damage from the explosion, and he had suffered critical injuries. The medical officer decided to put him into a hibernation healing chamber to prevent stress on his body as he healed.

Ben noticed his sister's distress and joined her to comfort her. "Hey, Katie, are you okay?"

She wiped a tear from her face as she turned, because she wanted to appear strong for her brother. "Yeah, I am good; just stress I guess. Ben, I miss Daddy."

Ben sighed. "I do too, sis. We all do. Hey, get out of here awhile. It will be later on before we start anyways. Jen called; she is about thirty minutes out. Go meet her at the docking bay."

Katie hugged her brother and agreed a walk would do her good. She left the briefing room, followed closely by Max and Shorty.

A short time later, she watched as the familiar *Lady Tiger* set down next to her own ship, *Vixen*. She excitedly stood by the door, waiting to see her big sister. The seal on the door broke with a hiss, and the ramp lowered. Jennifer walked down the steps to greet her sister, accompanied by their cousin.

The sisters hugged, and Katie spoke first. "I missed you!"

Jennifer returned the favor. "I missed you too, little sis!"

Katie pulled away from Jennifer to greet her cousin. "Breanna. I am glad you were able to get off Mars."

Breanna replied. "Yeah, I am too. Things are getting bad there. Those jerks in the government are getting scared of what you guys may do."

Jennifer interrupted. "Hey, girl, you are one of us now, and it is not what we may do, but what we will do."

Katie gestured for them to go, but the other two hesitated as they watched a quartet of small Earth fighters enter the bay.

Katie was curious as to why Earth fighters had arrived. She did not see anything on the station's reports about them. Jennifer and Breanna joined the first pilot. As the pilot removed her helmet, Katie immediately recognized her.

She thought aloud, "Anna Jo, Jen's friend from school." As the other female pilots climbed from their respective fighters, she recognized them as well. They had been members of Jennifer's basketball team in school. She remembered their teammates calling them the Fab Five. The tallest she knew was Keisha, the petite one was Shayna and last, but not least, was the one that had lived close to them, Lauren.

The group of young women approached her, and Jennifer introduced her little sister. "Guys, this is my little sis, Katie. She is the commander of this rock."

Keisha stepped forward and saluted.

"Commander Graham, we have come to join your fight against the Interstellar Alliance."

They exchanged quick greetings, and Katie gestured for the group to follow her. "Come on, ladies. The briefing is this way."

They reluctantly followed when they spotted Max. Jennifer grabbed the two closest to her. "Come on; he is okay. He is just a big fur ball."

As they approached Max, his gun pointed at each of them as he looked at them. He realized he had not deactivated it and quickly did so. Jennifer introduced him. "Ladies, this is our tiger friend, Max."

They gasped as he greeted them. "Hello, ladies."

Lauren and Shayna screamed. "He can talk!"

Jennifer laughed and said, "Sorry, I forgot to mention that."

The group walked down the hall toward the elevators.

Anna Jo asked, "Jennifer, tell us how is Max able to speak."

Jennifer began to explain to them how Max could talk as they walked along.

Katie followed a bit behind, feeling better than she had in a long time. Her big sis was back, and they soon would have her father back as well.

The Rescue Plan Begins

The group of young women arrived at the briefing room a short time later. As they entered, their laughter and joyful banter abruptly ended. A sense of urgency and seriousness met them inside as Ben and Dylan greeted them.

Ben was the only one to speak. "Welcome back, Jen. We are glad to have you back with us. We must get started. One of our agents on Mars has informed us of where they are holding Dad."

His youngest sister, Katie, excitedly responded to the news. "Where is he? When are we going to get him?"

Ben understood her feelings as he attempted to calm her. "Katie, it will be soon, I promise you that." Ben remembered something. "Oh, by the way, little sis, a call came for you on Shorty's code frequencies—seven I believe."

Katie excused herself and left the group, calling for her little friend, Shorty, to follow.

Ben whispered to his oldest sister. "It is her friend A. J. He got us the info, and he had really wanted to tell Katie the news. I told him to hold on."

Jennifer smiled as she gestured for her friends, who joined her and her brother.

Dylan excused himself as an aide called for him. "Excuse me; we can meet formally later."

Jennifer turned to each of them one by one to introduce her.

He knew the first one fairly well because she was related to him. "Hello, Breanna, did you have any trouble while on Earth?"

She responded in her ever-professional way. "No, everything went well. Sarah and her brother Lee are handling things professionally. The commander seems to think, although reluctant to join the fight, Earth may send us a ship or two."

Ben asked about their friend Bethany. "She was in the process of being released pending any further—"

Anna Jo interrupted. "Any further bad attitude."

Breanna glared at her friend with a look, as if to say shut up!

Jennifer took the interruption as an opening to introduce her friends from Earth. "These are my friends from school. They have come to join us."

As she said each name, they stepped forward to greet him: Keisha, Anna Jo, Lauren, and Shayna.

Ben spoke. "I'm glad you are here; we need all the help we can get."

The four of them replied together, "We are happy to be here."

The smallest member of the team spoke as Jennifer called a pilot over. "We are here to help you get your father back, sir."

The pilot was their cousin Jared. "Hi. I will get you up to speed on how we do things out here."

Keisha couldn't help but ask him about the patch below his name, and he replied proudly, "My guys gave me the call sign in flight school, and it stuck; besides I love my momma." He smiled at them. "You can call me Momma's Boy."

Dylan called to the group, "We need to get started. Our data is time sensitive, and we need to act fast."

Ben found a seat to relinquish the floor to his commander of special operations. The other in the room did as well and the planning of the rescue was underway, a rescue that all in the room felt was well overdue. Katie whispered to herself, "Dad, we are coming to get you soon."

Max had heard her and licked her hand.

The Confrontation

Many in the room had not slept in nearly twenty-four hours, and tension filled the air. Jennifer and Max stood worriedly watching the confrontation that occurred before them. Jennifer knew it would come sooner or later, because the two who stood before her as comrades were combatants only a short month ago.

The Sasquatch known as Big Buford yelled at the man only a few feet away. His language could be heard garbled with the translated static words. "I refrain from breaking your neck right here because my adopted sister Jennifer cares much for you."

Upon hearing the Sasquatch's threat, the mercenary robot known as Warrior moved closer to his friend Dalton, also known as the mercenary called Hawk. Rhino, the marine robot who had been assigned as Big Buford's bodyguard, matched the move and stood by his Sasquatch friend.

Ben ordered the room cleared in an attempt to lessen the tension because he knew the Sasquatch could sense human emotion and the less of them in the room the better. Those in the highest command roles remained, as well the female Sasquatch.

Katie sat with her Sasquatch sister Sasha, who appeared unaffected by the argument. Her bodyguard, the robotic marine Guardian, was not as calm and had moved closer to her side. Sasha whispered through her translation mask, "My brother will not harm him. He has respect for him, because despite the size difference between them, your friend does not back down. His role in our mother's death is well known, but Dalton has redeemed himself to us. He has fought by our side valiantly since that night."

Katie felt more at ease, enough to smile as she noticed Guardian move closer. She had seen Sasha in combat and knew that Sasha didn't need a bodyguard and that she only accepted the robot's protection to make Ben feel better. The two had become friends and were always at each other's side.

Katie was pulled from her thoughts by more shouting. Her sister, now between them, was shouting, "Stop it, both of you! We all have doubts about continuing the fight and all have reasons to continue to do so."

The Sasquatch orphans spoke as one. "We fight for revenge for our family and home world."

Dalton, known formally as the mercenary called Hawk, spoke. "I fight for redemption for deeds I have done on behalf of the Interstellar Alliance.

Ben spoke as he sat at the table. "Well, folks, looks like we need to talk. We need to decide right now if this fight is worth continuing. We will not leave this room until we are ready to fight or quit."

Dylan agreed and spoke. "I suggest we all need to tell how the Alliance has affected us and why we need to continue to fight it."

The Sasquatch male joined his sister, Sasha, as she spoke. "Since my brother and our story is the source of this confrontation here, we shall begin. Hawk's story is intertwined with ours."

Katie listened as she spoke, and her memory drifted back to the world known as Nebula One and that fatal night.

Ambush in Deep Space

The Sasquatch female had barely started her story when alarms bellowed aboard the space station, signaling the station was under attack. Katie jumped to her feet and from her thoughts.

An Interstellar Alliance fighter carrier had jumped from light speed and began launching its swarm of fighters. Confusion took hold of the small group but was brought under control as Ben yelled orders above the alarms. He signaled for a technical unit near the control station to silence the alarms, as they left the bridge conference room.

Katie noticed the Sasquatch siblings talking and the female left the bridge but didn't have time to give it much thought as she joined the others. She noticed that the large barge alongside had already begun attempts to harness the floating station. She could see the glow of the barge's plasma shield generator powering up. She thought aloud, "We will be safe from those fighters here."

Jennifer looked up from the view screen, where she monitored the launching fighters. "Those outside the shield won't be."

Jennifer worried about her friends and family in the fighters.

Ben yelled into the communication console. "*Sarah Elizabeth*, this is command. Your captain cannot make it out to you. Engage that fighter carrier and make your escape. We will meet you at the rendezvous point October."

Big Willie docked with *MS*-1023 with a loud clang, and a feeling of helplessness came over Breanna. She joined her cousins. Katie spoke to reassure her, "We are safe in here."

A voice from the speaker got her attention. "*MS*-1023 command, this is EF-0810. My group is ready to launch; deactivate the shield."

Katie looked at Ben for approval, and he gave in with a nod.

Katie turned to speak into the microphone, but her sister grabbed her arm. "Katie delay them a while, okay?"

Dylan heard her and commented, "Captain, we sure could use those fighters out there."

Jennifer yelled in frustration, "I know Dylan, I know!"

She grabbed her cousin Breanna and said, "Come on, let's help our friends."

As they left the command bridge, Jennifer spoke into her headset, "Deck officer, get JDF-0832 ready for launch."

Katie looked toward the door worriedly but did as her sister wished. "Earth force, this is command. The shield will be down in moments. Be careful out there."

A short time later, the two cousins ran into the hangar. A deck robot met them and handed each of them a flight suit. Their friends made impatient gestures at them. "Hey, Captain Graham, I didn't know you were a pilot."

Keisha waived from the nearest earth fighter. "Hey, Crazy Legs, you guys didn't think we were going to let you all go it by yourselves. I have learned to fly these things out of the need to survive out here."

Jennifer pointed toward the Jupiter-class fighter bomber to her left, and Breanna climbed into the rear seat. And she turned to wave as she heard a friendly voice in her ear. "Bre, I thought you were a battleship captain?"

As she buckled in, she replied to Lauren's remark, "Not today; my ship will be fighting without me."

Jennifer joined her and a short time later the small group began to launch.

Shayna was the first to launch. "Trigger is out. I am glad you two are along."

The others followed close behind. As Jennifer piloted her fighter bomber from the hangar, a robot fighter crashed into the station just a bit off her portside. Another was destroyed as the plasma shield reactivated.

Jennifer heard a familiar voice in her ear. "Welcome to the fight, Angels. Who is the leader of your group?"

The pilots screamed from the speaker as one. "Gumby is!"

Breanna laughed from the rear seat and made it unanimous. "Gumby is our leader, Momma's Boy."

Jennifer accepted the lead and began to take control. "Jared we need a sixth pilot."

Her cousin responded to her request. "Copy that Fighting Angels Leader. Rebel Four will join you."

"Copy that. Glad to have her. Oh, and I like the name too." Jennifer knew who the pilot was and smiled.

The Galaxy 12 fighter pilot joined them as Shayna and Lauren's fighters were engaged by Alliance fighters. "Rebel Four, you are with Crash and Trigger. Get over there, and give them a hand!" Jennifer screamed into her headset.

The galaxy-class fighter jerked to starboard and streaked to help the overwhelmed fighters. "My call sign is Valkyrie, by the way." Her voice was electronically altered to disguise her identity.

A few seconds later, a robotic cruiser exited light speed. Jennifer noticed the new arrival and spoke to her partner in the rear seat. "Arm the bombs. We got to take that thing out."

Breanna quickly did as she was told, while firing the rear gun turret.

The rebel fighters made many runs at the Alliance cruiser. Success was hard earned, with the passing of the minutes. A half hour passed, and tension grew.

The trio of fighters flew passed the battleship called *Sarah Elizabeth*, which had finished off the carrier and was moving to engage the cruiser. Her captain, Breanna gave the order for the ship to leave the battle. "*Sarah Elizabeth*, this is your captain. Get out of here."

The battleship proceeded to carry out the order without question.

A few seconds later, Katie's voice sounded in Jennifer's ear. "Jennifer, we are ready to leave; we cannot do much to help. Take out that cruiser and get out of here before any more arrive."

She responded confidently as not to worry her little sister. "Roger that, commander I understand. We will see you later."

Dylan joined the conversation. "We have launched attack shuttles and med shuttles to assist you."

Jennifer dodged enemy fighters as her wing pilots, Anna Jo and Keisha, attempted to clear a path through a swarm of fighters. Breanna yelled, "Bombs have hit their marks!"

Jennifer looked up from the explosion below them in time to see *Big Willie* and *MS*-1023 jump to light speed and safety. A couple other bombers hit the cruiser, and it began to break apart.

The order to retreat came after a few more fighters made strafing runs across the cruiser's hull. "All fighters, this is Rebel Leader. Jump to light speed as soon as you can."

The remaining fighters formed up for the jump.

The pilots of the Fighting Angels group called out, "Crash is here. Crazy Legs is here. Terminator is here. Trigger is here. Valkyrie is here."

Jennifer responded to her group. "Gumby and Bre are here. Glad you all made it, and good job." Jared joined the conversation as several of his fighters took out a few remaining enemy fighters and began to jump. "Good job Angels. Let's get out of here."

Keisha jumped in. "Jared, I would like to make a quick request."

"Make it quick."

"Copy that. We would like for Valkyrie to join our group."

Jared replied with hesitation in his voice. "She is one of my best pilots." He asked his pilot, "What you think, you want to join these greenies?"

The young female quickly answered her commander, with her electronically altered voice. "Sir, it would be an honor to serve with these ladies. Sure, they may be a little green, but they can fight."

Before he jumped, Jared gave one last order, "Rebel four, you are officially transferred to the Fighting Angels squad. See you all at the rendezvous."

Jared's fighter jumped and was gone; the Fighting Angels followed close behind.

Jennifer and Breanna were alone in light speed and rode quietly. Breanna broke the silence. "I have been thinking, I would like to relinquish command of the *Sarah Elizabeth* and join the Fighting Angels."

Jennifer sat quietly listening as her cousin spoke.

"I like this hunk of metal we are in. Although I have been back here, I feel this ship is a part of me, and I have control of my contribution to the fight more in here."

Jennifer laughed and spoke, "Hey you cannot have my ship."

They laughed, and Breanna continued, "I don't want your ship, just one like her. I thought about getting Ben to program one of the marine units, like Guardian, as a gunner."

Jennifer responded seriously, "You have thought about it a lot, and I think it is cool, and on second thought, you can have my ship. I will help you talk to Ben and Dylan. Kind of sounds great, doesn't it? Breanna the fighter pilot, cool. Besides, Bethany can resume command of *Sarah Elizabeth* when she returns."

After about a minute of thinking, Breanna spoke again, "Jen, I will stay in command of the *Sarah Elizabeth* until Bethany returns."

Jennifer replied from the front seat, "That's cool; we really need a good leader on her bridge right now."

The young women spent the remainder of the jump relaxing.

The Dream

Jennifer and Breanna took advantage of their trip in light speed to catch up on some much-needed rest, by setting the fighter bomber's life support system to put them into a temporary hibernation cycle.

The deep slumber brought an unwelcome dream of the past to Jennifer's mind. One filled with horror.

An explosion rocked the Mars University on the moon Phobos.

Chaotic noise and the smell of smoke greeted Jennifer as she regained consciousness. She saw her mother lying on the floor nearby, with her large blue-robed robotic guard standing over her. Jennifer crawled immediately to her side, ignoring the pain in her knee. She pushed her mother's aide away and took her mother in her arms.

"Mom, are you okay?"

A moment later her mother spoke, coughing as blood fell from her lips. "Jen, I think I am going to die."

She took her daughter's hand in her bloodstained hands. Jennifer could see how bad her mother was injured. Jennifer screamed at the aide to get help.

The aide sadly responded, "I am sorry; we have called for help, but there is a battle with terrorists, and the medical units are unable to reach us."

Jennifer held her mother helplessly.

Jennifer was startled as the guard unit standing over them began firing his laser gun and spoke in a mechanical voice. "We have trouble here!"

Two shots later a pair of terrorists lay dead only fifty feet away.

Jennifer looked at her mother once more as if to ask what she should do. Her mother spoke with a crackling voice, "Jen, get out of here. Tell your brother and sister I love them."

Jennifer began to sob as her mother drooped lifeless in her arms.

She jerked as the aide grabbed her to help her to her feet. Then he fell to the ground as the blast from an enemy rifle found its mark. Without thinking, Jennifer scampered to her feet, grabbing his weapon. She felt she had no friends left, until she looked into the robotic guard's mechanical face. He spoke calmly and reassuringly, "We must get out of her."

Jennifer smiled sadly and spoke as she looked one last time at her mother. "We can use the escape pods."

The pair headed toward the escape pod bay but hesitated when a familiar voice called from the nearby debris, "Jennifer, help me!"

She and her new friend were at Professor Alexander Maxamillion's side in seconds.

The older man knelt by the pregnant Bengal tiger, Sheba. Tears filled Jennifer's eyes when she realized the beautiful beast was dead. Her friend Maxamillion touched her shoulder to comfort her. "We need to get her cubs out; the sensor shows faint life signs." Jennifer quickly shuffled through the med kit in his bag for a surgical knife because she knew a laser scalpel was too dangerous.

As she returned to the task at hand, she noticed that her friend was injured and bleeding.

He grabbed her hand as she reached for his abdomen. "Do not worry about me; I am okay. We do not have much time."

He showed her where to cut, and Jennifer used the knife with confidence and skill. She thought of how well the man next to her had taught her. She took hold of the first cub and was overcome with sadness when she felt its lifeless little body. She noticed motion from the mother tiger's body and quickly retrieved the little male cub. She tied off the cord as Professor Maxamillion instructed and they shared a moment of happiness in the horror that surrounded them.

The professor spoke firmly to her. "This little guy needs medical attention; you must get him out of here."

She dumped out her backpack and put the trembling little tiger inside, wrapped in one of her sweaters. As she turned to Alexander to help him to his feet, she saw him lying over Sheba's body, lifeless as well.

She screamed, "When is this madness going to end!"

Her mourning for her friend was cut short by more laser fire in the distance. She gestured to her robotic companion and spoke, "The pod bay is this way."

The two were soon in a pod and a bit later safe aboard the diplomat cruiser *Sword of Orion*. Jennifer held the small tiger in her arms and spoke softly. "I'll call you, Max."

The alarm sounded in the cockpit, waking Jennifer and Breanna. Jennifer spoke to herself with the dream still in her mind, "That is why I need to continue the fight."

Her cousin asked from the seat behind. "What? Did you say something, Jen?"

Jennifer spoke, rubbing the sleep from her eyes. "Nothing, I am just thinking out loud."

The two remained silent as they flew on to their destination.

The Birth of a Friendship

Dylan was tired of tinkering around on his ship, the *Saber II,* and decided to check on his friend Tyton. He touched the data cable attached to his mechanical friend. The techs said they were attempting to reboot his personality program, and the computer link was the last hope.

The door opened, and he turned as Ben and Shorty entered. Ben spoke as he picked up a tool from the table. "I got an idea. Shorty here has become one of our best computer experts lately. He may be able to fix our friend here."

The little robot whistled confidently, and Ben and Dylan laughed.

Dylan looked at the monitor as schematics of the Tyton series marine unit appeared. He spoke as he pulled a chair up beside Shorty. "Well the little guy seems to know what he is doing; it is worth a shot."

He patted the robot as he sat down. "Hey, did I ever tell you how the big guy and I met?"

Ben shrugged his shoulders. "Only that you met in combat onboard one of the old Earth defense platforms. You really didn't go into much detail."

Dylan pulled a chair next to him with his foot. "Well, now is a good time. It will take the little guy awhile."

Ben joined his friend, eager to know how the bond between the man and robot became so strong.

Dylan began his story the way a lot of war veterans did.

The group of Mars transports approached the defense platform on the moon Phobos, which had been central command for Earth force stationed in the system.

"I sat with my unit aboard our transport, *Lancer*. I remember feeling more nervous than I had felt during the conflict because Mars command had decided to send a squad of their new Tyton series marines along.

Ben asked curiously, "Was Tyton on your transport?"

Dylan looked toward his friend on the table next to them and sighed. "You know, I am not sure. I can only remember looking across at the emotionless mechanical face of the unit across from me."

Dylan paused a second or two as if to regain his composure. Scratching his head, he resumed his story. "I was glad the trip to the deck was a short one because those things freaked me out, and I remember being angry at my commanders because I was about to be in combat and did not need to be feeling that way. I needed to have confidence in the troops with me."

Ben interrupted him, kind of confused. "You sound like you hated mechanicals back then. It is hard to picture, after what I witnessed at the Uranus factory."

The elder of the two sighed. "Are you going to let me tell this story or not? I am not good at this stuff anyways. I did not really hate them; I had not served directly with them in combat. My opinion of those large buckets quickly changed when we hit the deck. The group on the Lancer secured the landing bay in a few seconds."

Ben looked at him with disbelief, and his friend shuffled in his chair. "Well, okay, I said it seemed to be seconds; it was longer. I was still a short time."

Ben noticed that his friend was having trouble as he stood by his mechanical friend. His leg seemed to bother him more since they had begun fighting the Alliance.

"We needed to take the facility intact that is why we needed feet on the ground. The fighting was intense, and resistance was strong. I took command when our leader went down. And it wasn't long before my quad vehicle took a hit, my driver was killed, and I was thrown from the gun seat, as another blast took out an overhead support, pinning me to the floor and knocking me out. When I awoke I felt the pain in my leg. I heard the medic say it was severely broken, and he called for help. One of the mechanical marines arrived and pulled the beam off my leg and literally carried me out of the main combat area.

"The next thing I remember was waking up with that same mechanical marine standing guard by my bed. The nurse that was there said he had remained at my side since he brought me in. She said she had never seen loyalty in a mechanical like that before. I asked around and no one else could explain it because no other mechanical marine unit had acted like that.

"He stayed with me until I went into surgery, and after I came out he was gone and I never saw him again. When I joined intelligence, I tracked him down; and since the series had been taken out of service after the war, I requisitioned it for intelligence recon and later bought him.

"I gave him the name Tyton after the series, and that is what we affectionately call him today. He never left my side, and that is why I will not leave his. That is why I call him friend."

A call for Ben from the command center interrupted, and Ben had to leave. "He has become a friend to us all. Let me know if anything changes."

Ben left his friends to see what was up.

The memory of the battle and how he was injured made Dylan's leg ache. He rubbed it in an attempt to ease the pain as he looked at his fallen friend. He became angry as he thought of how he fought for an Interstellar Alliance's government, which now he now knew was corrupt and deceitful from the start of the Mars War, and that he would suffer a constant and nagging pain from the injury he sustained in that fight. He whispered to himself, "That is why I need to continue to fight."

Shorty whistled, and he looked at the monitor beside the bed and smiled. Shorty had done what the techs could not. Tyton's memory and personality programs had begun a long reboot cycle. Excited, Dylan patted the little robot and said, "Thanks, little guy, and you did a good job."

An Unexpected Ally

The members of the Fighting Angels squad waited in the docking bay after hearing the news that the two remaining members of the unit were landing soon.

The pilot known as Valkyrie climbed from her fighter and joined Jennifer and Breanna. As the trio walked to greet the others, Jennifer gestured for the mysterious pilot to keep her helmet on until they were close to the others. A few moments later and after all greetings were finished, Valkyrie removed her helmet. Shock and surprise engulfed the group.

Anna Jo screamed aloud, "Jessica! What the heck are you doing out here, and a rebel pilot no doubt!"

Jennifer rushed to silence her surprised friend before she could say Jessica's last name aloud. "Terminator, keep it down.

We must keep Jess's identity a secret because if the Alliance gets news that she is with us, her father may be killed."

Breanna asked curiously about why her friend's voice sounded different.

Jessica replied touching her throat, "I was injured during my last combat mission when my fighter took a hit, causing a section of my control panel to blow up sending shrapnel into my throat. The medic is not sure if my voice will ever be the same."

The small group of friends began to catch up when they were interrupted by a call over the speakers in the landing bay. "The command group is needed in the command center! Repeat: command group is needed in the command center!"

Jennifer spoke quietly as she stood to leave. "Well, I got to get to work. Oh, I have one other thing to say before we go." She gestured for Breanna to join her. "Breanna will be joining your squadron when Bethany returns from Earth."

The pair walked away, leaving surprise in their wake.

They were directed to the conference room as they entered the command center. Jennifer was surprised when she saw Tyton standing near the door. She greeted him as she found a seat. "Good to see you are back with us, Tyton."

He replied in his familiar voice, "It is good to be back. The little blue guy there got me working again."

Jennifer smiled at Shorty.

Dylan took the floor. "As many of you know, we moved Panther to another facility for continued treatment."

Jennifer spoke up. "Where did he go? Breanna and I just got back."

Ben answered his sister's question. "He was taken by Sasha and her brother to rendezvous with a Sasquatch medical ship in the outer rim of the solar system; the location is classified. Only the medical staff knows, for security reasons."

Ben continued to explain. "The Sasquatch doctors are attempting to use cloning technology they have to reconstruct several of his damaged organs; this should speed up his recovery considerably."

The nearby technician spoke. "Sir, we need to proceed. The longer we keep the connection, we are risking detection."

Jennifer apologized and instructed him to proceed.

The incoming message was preceded by the Prime Minister of Mars' insignia, causing a murmur to fill the small room. Silence took hold as Mars' Prime Minister appeared, flanked by two well-known rebels. He began to address the small group. "Hello Commander Graham, my name is Logan; few of you know me. As for those that do not, I am the prime minister of the colony on Mars. I am accompanied by the robotic captain of the *Tiger's Pride*, and one of your best agents on Mars as proof that what I am about to say is legitimate."

Logan continued, "Your agent Aaron is why I am speaking with you today. You see, a few months ago, he brought the corruption that exists in the Interstellar Alliance to my attention. I am sorry it took so long to contact you, but I needed to keep my intentions secret. As you know, several of my friends in the government were executed for their opposition to the Alliance's Chancellor and his cabinet members.

"With your agents' help, I found allies within what is left of Mars's defense fleet. We have been able to gather a fleet of twelve ships. As you will find out it is a ragtag but capable fleet. My captains assure me the ships are ready and able to fight. Well, all but two; the medical frigate *Pride of Kentucky* and the battle cruiser *Peabody* had to literally fight their way out of Alliance-controlled space. I am told by your technicians here at Neptune they will get them in shape as soon as possible."

Katie, the smallest of the group, stood as tall as she could and addressed the Prime Minister. "We welcome your aid because as you probably know we are in a tough fight out here."

As he acknowledged her gratitude, she sat down to silently listen to what else he had to say. The Prime Minister's voice deepened with despair. "I bring you grave news as well. The Alliance's mechanical soldiers have seized Mars's terra-forming generators. We have learned they intend to modify them to create a planetary shield, and if allowed to be activated no one will be able to enter or leave the planet. As for an assault on the planet, it would be impossible. I hope, Commander Graham, you find something helpful in the data your youngest sister obtained during her mission to Mars awhile back. I will talk more when we meet. Good luck to you all."

Before the transmission ended, Mech 1 spoke to his captain. "Captain Graham, your ship is ready; we are scheduled to leave the Neptune system within the hour."

The screen went black, and despair filled the room. Katie spoke solemnly, "Guys, we need to get to Dad soon."

Farewell to a Friend

The meeting lasted a short time longer, and after it ended, Jennifer went to find her friend Dalton.

She found him in the hangar bay working on his ship called *Stinger*. As she approached him she could hear him talking to a maintenance robot. "Captain Hawk, here is your fighter, and it has been repaired to your specs."

Without looking from his work, he responded, "Leave it by my ship. I will mount it myself. Thanks."

Jennifer spoke to him. "Hey, you need help?"

He looked in her direction and smiled. "Sure, grab the controls of the lift and move *Cub* under here." Jennifer did as he had asked, and Dalton hooked the small fighter onto the clamps beneath the ship.

The two sat on a nearby container, and he spoke, while wiping his brow. "Jen, I am leaving."

She looked at him sadly. "Why? I thought you were staying."

Her friend stood and looked away. "I was, but I am having a hard time dealing with what happened on Nebula One."

He leaned against *Stinger* and began to explain, "I and my partner are the reason why the Sasquatch orphans' mother is dead.

"The events of that night started out as a just another job. My partners, Warrior and Scorpion, and I were hired by the Alliance's Chancellor to conduct what I thought was a recon mission on the planet. We were in the hills near what we determined to be the capital when we spotted Katie's ship and a Sasquatch gunship fly over."

Jennifer spoke, "We met with Panther's contacts on one of the moons, but Sasha and Buford's father sent their mother and them to the planet. He knew it would be safer there when the Alliance fleet arrived."

Dalton looked up as Warrior came out of their ship and stood by them. "Scorpion got a signal from the Alliance fleet that arrived shortly after, and he informed Warrior and me what our real job was. We had been sent there to disable any planetary defenses. The fleet had arrived early, and we were unable to do so, and the attempt by the Interstellar Alliance to take the planet failed."

A look of regret in his eyes caused Jennifer to feel sad for her friend because she knew how Dalton felt about his involvement in their Sasquatch friend's family's death. She spoke solemnly. "Buford and Sasha's father and brothers were killed in the battle in orbit above the planet."

He agreed with her, with a bit of crackle in his voice. "I know. I learned about that when I arrived here. I guess I am lucky I am still alive too. The Sasquatch is a strong species and capable warriors. I have learned that when confronting an adversary any sign of weakness could mean death. I believe that lesson is why I survived my first meeting with them."

He spoke seriously to her again. "Jennifer, that is one of the reasons I must leave; the tension is high when I am near them. I will end up getting killed or killing one of them."

He returned to his story of that evening on Nebula One. "When we failed, Scorpion began to get irate because he said that the Chancellor would not pay us. We had a lot of expenses tied up in that job. We were about to pull out when he realized that it was Katie's ship *Vixen* that we had seen landing. He wanted to go after you for the bounty on you." He paused a few seconds.

"Warrior and I just wanted to get out of there, but Scorpion took us in when we had no other place to go after my parents were killed in a crash after pirates attacked our freighter *Lynx* near Ceres City on the dwarf planet Ceres. Warrior and I escaped aboard my little ship *Cub*, but my parents were unable to get out. We went along with his plan out of a sense of debt, I guess."

"We stayed behind, to keep you two under surveillance while he went back to *Stinger* for more supplies. While he was gone, I expressed to Warrior that I did not like his plan to go after you guys and that I just wanted to get out of there."

He looked at Warrior, and the robot added, "I agreed to do whatever he decided." The large robot gestured to his friend.

A message came over his arm communication's device, and Jennifer listened close. "Captain Hawk, we have been ordered to move up your departure time."

He responded, "Roger. Hangar Control, I am ready to go whenever you say."

Jennifer spoke into her headset unit. "Command, can you give Dalton a few more minutes?"

A familiar voice of one of the command center officers responded, "Captain Graham, he has about thirty minutes. The commander has ordered the station to relocate. She wants any ship that is scheduled leave to be off the station before we dock with the barge."

Dalton sighed. "I guess I had better wrap my story up. "We tracked you to where you two had gone, and as you know, a fight began. Scorpion was the first to engage; he took out the guards that were outside. When we entered the compound, we found Sasha and her mother, who put up a fight. He killed her mother and went for her when Max came in and jumped him, injuring him. I had Warrior carry him, and we retreated to a secure location."

Jennifer spoke again. "I remember when we got into the room Sasha was furious and the guards had difficulty getting her to leave. Her brother Buford arrived and convinced her to go below ground."

Dalton choked up as he began to continue. "I saw my mentor angrier than I had seen him before. He was filled with rage and was determined to collect the bounty on you two. He treated his wounds himself and started to go after you. He made the statement that he would kill you if he had to."

He placed his hand on hers. "You are one of my dearest friends and were always good to me when others were not. I could not let him go through with his plans. Warrior and I attempted once more to convince him to leave but failed to do so. He started to leave, and I confronted him; and in anger he pulled his gun and fired. I returned fire and missed, but Warrior did not. My mentor and friend lay dead on the ground, and shock and despair took hold of me. Warrior quickly took control and got us out of there, just ahead of the Sasquatch soldiers. Our escape was cut short by your ship *Tiger's Pride*."

Jennifer smiled at him. "After a short time and a bit of persuasion, you joined us. And you made your peace with the orphans and even earned their respect too."

He spoke softly. "Tension still remains. You saw it the other day."

A short silence between them was broken by Max who had come looking for Jennifer.

Dalton stood and sighed. "Well, I guess I need to get going. I need to deal with things on my own. Scorpion may have been hard and cruel at times, but he was all I had. He is why I am alive today; he taught me what I know. He was a mercenary, and I am one too. I am the mercenary known to everyone as Hawk. That name gives me an identity and a purpose. This fight is not my fight. I wish you luck; we are going to our base in the Kuiper Belt. We really need to go."

He hugged his friend and boarded his ship. He gave his robotic partner the command to power up the ships drive engines. He called out to the deck robot. "Tell them I am ready to leave."

He looked one last time at his friend who had begun to cry.

She yelled to him. "Good-bye. You take care of yourself."

He hit the button to close the hatch and said good-bye. The hatch shut with a hissing sound.

A short time later *Stinger* was gone with her friend aboard, its destination somewhere in the outer edge of the solar system. Jennifer left the hangar sad. She knew she couldn't let the emotion take hold of her because she had things to do. She had to rescue her dad.

Deceptions Discovered

Ben and Katie fought sleep as they continued to scan the files retrieved on her mission to Mars. Their little blue companion, Shorty, worked faithfully by their sides. He checked each file as they finished them. His computer brain was more likely to catch hidden data that tired human eyes may miss.

Katie smiled as she discovered the program that was responsible for the puppy dog glitch. She whispered to Shorty. "This I why you are like you are."

She saved it to a small storage device and passed it to the little blue robot. Shorty secured it in a compartment as Katie deleted the original file in the data.

Ben became more alert when he discovered a file about his cybernetic research. The first data stream to process was his grades from high school, especially his technology courses. He whispered to himself, "Why does the Alliance still have my transcript?"

He read on, more curious now.

A few pages later, a deception revealed itself to him: cybernetic technology project for new soldiers. He read on and discovered a document authorizing a project called Cybernetic Soldier Project using his own research in the field. He thought to himself, *That is why I got my money for school; the Alliance was looking for a scientist they could recruit or technology they could steal.*

He showed what he had found to his sister. He spoke a bit angry. "Well, I guess I have my reason to continue to fight the Alliance. I did not get into cybernetics to create weapons. I did it to help people to adapt and survive out here in the colonies."

Katie wondered if her name would come up in the data, so she instructed Shorty to do a scan for data matches under her name, and short time later, something appeared. It was a note from the finance director of the Interstellar Alliance to the Chancellor.

> I have just received a grant proposal from a young woman in the astronomy field. I feel she and her knowledge would be useful in our discovery of any habitable planets we could exploit. I suggest we process her grant without haste. I see she was aided in her proposal by Mr. Chayce Joseph Jackson an officer in our research fleet. He is known to his friends

> and close associates as Boots. This could be an opportunity to get him out of the way. Our intelligence agency has determined him as a threat to or plans.

Katie looked at her brother and remarked, "Well, Ben, we have found reason to continue the fight, reasons we can add to those we already have."

Shorty interrupted them with erratic whistles and beeps. The data that appeared was exactly what they had been searching for. Katie sighed with exhaustion as she read about a plan for a planetary shield using terra-forming generators.

"Katie, we need to get some sleep. We can bring this to the others tomorrow," Ben said to his little sister. He called for a tech unit, and after it arrived, he spoke as they left the room. "Help the little guy get this data ready."

The robot responded as the door shut. "Yes, I will have it done as you asked."

Battle Group Assembled (Mars' Freedom)

Ben asked his long-time friend Dylan to meet with him before joining the others. Ben stood looking out the view-port at the fleet of warships assembled. Dylan's greeting echoed inside the large storage chamber. "What is up?"

"I just want to thank you for all your help. I know you were not looking for another fight when we started our adventures together."

Dylan responded by saying, "I kind of saw it was coming; you know, the rebellion. I was a marine and will always be a marine. We are trained to fight and never run from one. What is on your mind?"

Ben began to speak once more with stress in his voice. "I am tired of fighting, and we cannot wait for any more help. It is time we take Mars. The regime in power there is a fanatical and dangerous one. I am going to order our attack on Mars to start today."

His friend agreed as he informed him of the morning's events. "I thought you would, so we have a plan ready. Earth is understandably sitting this one out. Bethany returned late last night with Sarah and her brother Lee." He continued with a bit of good news. "The commander was, however, able to convince the Earth government to send a couple of Special Forces squads. He has agreed to command them; they have already been briefed and are in route to Mars to attempt to rescue your father and should be ready when we arrive. I met with the Logan, and he assured me that his fleet is ready, with the exception of the two ships he mentioned the other day. He has turned command of them over to you. Bethany has returned to command of her ship, *Sarah Elizabeth*; and Breanna has joined her squad, the Fighting Angels aboard the fighter carrier *Monitor*. She and Jared have will be leading the fighters."

Ben looked at his friend a bit surprised and was greeted with a smile.

"I have been busy while you and Katie slept in. I met with the others after I was informed of what you two found last night. We got right on a plan for the attack, because we knew you would want to get started."

Ben laughed and headed for the door, with Dylan close behind.

He continued to brief his commander and friend. "I spoke with Jennifer and Katie before I came to see you, and they have moved the command center to the *Tiger's Pride*. They want you to join them there."

Ben stopped a second and asked, "What about the station?"

The older of the two spoke as he began to walk. "Your youngest sister brought up the idea of abandoning it; she thinks it will be dead weight. I think she feels what happened to *Big Rock* may happen." The two of them shared the memory of that tragic day, when their friends William and Boots were lost.

"Since the upgrades on that old barge are complete and she feels it would be better as a fighting ship than a babysitter, Mech 1 has assumed command of it."

Dylan chuckled a bit. "Katie renamed it, and we all feel it appropriate."

Ben looked at him. "She called it *Willie's Wrath*. Also the Sasquatch orphans will be leading a trio of their gunships, which Sasha convinced Nebula One's leaders to send."

Ben asked his friend and partner as they walked toward the hangar, "And what is your part in this plan?"

"Oh! I was getting to that. Tyton and I will be taking a group of attack transports. I found the Lancer, and she is still in good shape and is ready to fight. You didn't think I was staying behind did you?"

As they entered the hangar, Ben expressed his concern about not having enough medical frigates as a somewhat familiar voice interrupted them. Ben turned to see Panther, and as he removed his helmet Ben noticed immediately the yellow of his cybernetic eyes. He took his friend's hand and greeted him. "It is great to see you. Panther, how are you feeling?"

The older man responded, "I am good. The Sasquatch doctors have treated me well, and their cloning technology may put you out of business."

Ben smiled. "It sounds good to me. I prefer flesh to cybernetics; I am a biologist too."

He gestured to Panther's eyes, and the older man responded proudly. "They wanted to replace my eyes, but those cyber/techs in the Alliance didn't leave any tissue they could use. Hell, I had bad eyes anyways. Besides, cybernetic ones give me better night vision and heat detection capabilities."

Ben asked one last question, "Panther, I am sure you have been briefed. You want to take command?"

The older man responded quickly, "No, young man, it is yours and your sisters'. Besides, the Sasquatch doctor wants me to remain aboard the medical ship. I can monitor the battle from there and give input if needed. Let's go get your dad."

Ben said farewell to his old friend. As he boarded the shuttle, he said, "Looks like we will have another medical ship after all, but you knew that already." His friend smiled and said good-bye and left to board his attack transport.

A few short moments later, he was aboard his sister's ship, *Tiger's Pride*; and after a short elevator ride, he joined his siblings. Jennifer gestured to her seat, and he responded respectfully. "No way, Jennifer, this is your ship."

He went to the control pit to the right of the captain's chair. "I will command the battle from here."

The little robot known as Shorty joined him and connected to a console where he would be able to monitor battle tactics. Ben looked at their smallest companion and spoke, "I need you to find the robotic fleet's main control ship as soon as we exit light speed."

Ben looked at his sisters one last time before giving the order to begin the mission code named Mars's Freedom. Max walked over and laid down next to Jennifer's chair. Katie spoke as she watched the fleet jump to light speed. "Daddy, we are coming to get you!" A moment later the *Tiger's Pride* jumped to light speed.

A short time later the battle to liberate Mars and a rescue mission began.

War's End

The battle to end the war and liberate the planet Mars had lasted only a few hours. Although the rebellion had achieved victory, it had not come without loses and hardship.

The old battle cruiser known as *Tiger's Pride* drifted powerless in orbit above the planet, because it's main reactor had sustained damage during the battle.

The rebellion's command ship had been luckier than most in the fleet. The warship *Sarah Elizabeth* had been literally torn apart by constant bombardment from the Interstellar Alliance's robotic fighters. Her captain, Bethany, had barely escaped the battered ship and had been ordered to report to the medical frigate *Pride of Kentucky,* which had joined the battle late, for treatment, for her injuries. Her sister ship the *Peabody* had also arrived late. The two ships' late arrival was a major factor in the rebellion's success.

The reactor of the fallen *Sarah Elizabeth* had suffered no damage and had been retrieved to replace the one onboard its sister ship.

Jennifer shivered as she leaned over the control panel as she monitored the repair work on her ship. The emergency heaters on the bridge fought hard to keep the coldness of space from overtaking her. She thought about how she appreciated her grandfather Benard's design. He had designed the earlier warships for the Interstellar Alliance, back before the war with Earth. She smiled as she remembered how he had fought the government for compatibility between the different ship designs, a design feature that had served the Alliance well during the Mars War and made it easier to get her ship repaired now.

Mech 1 startled her as he patted her shoulder. "Captain, here is your arctic gear. I suggest you put it on, and you need to put on the life support gear as well. The oxygen levels are getting low." Jennifer thanked her robotic friend and hurried to get into the gear. As she put her coat on, her robotic friend spoke again.

"Captain, why did you not leave with the others and let the mechanicals do the repairs? She sat in a nearby seat and began to explain why she had disobeyed her brother's order to evacuate the ship.

"Big guy, you have been by my side since mom's death and you know me as well as my siblings. Did you notice how Ben didn't push me when I did not want to leave?" Her loyal friend shook his head in response.

"He knew I needed to make a stand right here on this bridge. This ship is the last thing the Alliance had not taken from my family. It took Katie's work and dream when we lost *Big Rock*. We lost our mother and they attempted to take Ben's work as well. We lost dear friends when William and Boots died too. Last, but not least they had our father." She stood and went to her captain's chair and pulled a plaque from underneath it.

Mech 1 took it and read it. "Battle cruiser 0001 is dedicated to and named in honor of Benard Edward Graham for his service to the Interstellar Alliance." Jennifer took it from him and placed it back underneath her chair and a tear fell from her eye. "This is the last thing I have from my grandfather. I discovered it was in the inventory of Falcon Intergalactic and was scheduled to be dismantled if not sold at the last company auction. I asked Willie to help me get it and he did. That is why we are under contracts with the company. We thought it was destroyed during the Mars War, but it got lost in the government bureaucracy."

A signal from the control panel interrupted them and the two went to check it out. Jennifer hit a button and a message flashed on the monitor. "The capital has been taken and we have control of the planet. I would also like to add the ARES compound has been destroyed and all survivors have been taken into custody. The Chancellor of the Interstellar Alliance is dead. I have personally confirmed it. The war is over!" The message was signed by Commander Graham.

She screamed aloud and quickly regained her composer. “We need to get this command ship up and running. We must secure the territory around the planet. I want to make sure that this is truly the war’s end.”

Reunion with Dad

The *Wrath of Willie* returned to Mars with the asteroid station MS-1023, which it had been ordered to retrieve. Ben and Logan had agreed it would be the best place to set up Mars' orbital command.

Jennifer watched as the tug drones moved her ship near the station, because its reactor had not been powered up. A short time later the docking tower's tractor beams activated and directed the large ship to one of the docking ports. She smiled as she saw the numerous ships approaching, the most recognizable one being her sister's ship *Vixen*.

Her little sister was to assume command of the station once more. Ben and Logan had asked her if she would also accept the leadership of Mars Orbital Command and she had accepted. Jennifer wondered how it would feel calling her baby sis General. Jennifer herself had reluctantly assumed a command role as well. Logan and a few other officials had asked her to take command of the emerging government's, The Solar Alliance's, fleet.

The station's static computer voice brought her out of her thoughts and turned her attention back towards the control panel. It repeated when she didn't respond immediately. "Docking complete, you may disembark at this time." Jennifer acknowledged the message and spoke into the microphone, although a vocal response was unnecessary. "Copy that MS-1023; I will be there when the General arrives."

Katie's voice blared from the speaker. "Hey, come on down and meet me in the command center. I know you do not have the heat on yet on that bucket of yours." She did not respond to her little sister, but turned and headed for the emergency ladder.

A short time later they exchanged greetings in the familiar surroundings of the station's command center. Jennifer's tiger companion, Max was there too, he had accompanied Katie on her flight over from Phobos.

After a short silence Katie asked. "How are repairs on your ship going?" Jennifer sighed as she responded. "They are complete and Mech-1 is checking all the systems before we activate the reactor from the *Sarah Elizabeth.* I have spent the last couple days freezing my butt off, but we got her fixed." Katie could not help but laugh. "Grandpa would be proud of you."

A signal from hanger control interrupted them. "General, your father is on his way in." The young women did not respond. They just screamed and headed for the door, followed by Max. As the two left, the communications officer responded on their behalf. "General Graham is on her way hanger control."

The sisters had not seen their father yet because the Earth Special Forces, had taken him to the *Pride of Kentucky* for treatment. After they had rescued him from the ARES facility, William's nephew had reported the facility had been destroyed during the rescue.

The two had arrived just as the Earth gunship set down on the deck followed by the escort fighters from Fighting Angel squadron.

Katie jumped up and down, uncontrollable as she waited for the hatch to open. A few seconds later she and her sister were in their father Benny's arms. "Dad we are so glad you are ok. We tried so many times to get to you."

Benny comforted his daughters. "I am okay. I have been through worse. Ben does want me to see a psychologist when we determine who we can trust."

A pair of Earth commando approached them and the closest to them spoke. "Well, ladies, our mission here is complete and we have been ordered back to Earth. I speak for my soldiers. We are all glad to help in rescuing your father." The sisters thanked him and said goodbye. As the two soldiers turned to leave Benny thanked them one last time. The Sergeant smiled and spoke quietly in his ear. "Your kids are really the ones who deserve thanks; they have earned respect from us all."

The girls of Fighting Angels Squadron ran past the commandos to join their friends. Anna Jo spoke as she passed them. "Sergeant we will be with you guys when our fighters are ready." The group was chaotic and Benny excused himself when he noticed Panther exit a nearby gunship. "Jen, I'll leave you girls alone."

Jennifer pulled her friend Anna Jo to the side. "Why are you all leaving?"

Her friend answered sadly, "We are part of Earth Fighter Defense and our fighters are owned by Earth."

Jennifer asked concerned. "You guys won't get in trouble will you?"

Their friend Jessica jumped in between them, scaring them. "They are not going to get into trouble Jen." Anna Jo winked and smiled. Jessica continued. "My dad asked Earth awhile back if they could help you guys out. That is why he got locked up."

Lauren spoke up as she joined them, with the others behind her. "We have been assigned to the Earth carrier Crimson Angel which was ordered to join the fight the other day. It now will be arriving next week with its battle group due to the end of the fighting."

Katie got a call from hangar control that Ben's ship was on final approach and she said a quick good-bye to join her father. Jennifer held back to say goodbye to her friends and joined them as Ben's ship entered the hangar.

Ben joined his father and his sisters shortly after his ship set down. Benny embraced his son and spoke into his ear, "Son I am proud of you and want to thank you for getting me out of that place."

Ben held on a short time and pulled away to speak. "It was my pleasure and I am glad to see you are ok. I also would like to return command of the Panthers to you at this time."

Benny looked at his friend Panther, who nodded his head. Benny stood straight as his aching back would allow. "I respectfully deny. Ben it is yours and Dylan's unit now."

Benny took his youngest daughters hand and said. "Will you excuse us Panther? I would like to spend awhile with my kids."

They walked towards the door and the man called Panther looked at them with respect. He knew the loss of his friends William and Boots would not be in vain.

The tiger Max stood by his side watching them leave not sure if he should follow. Jennifer turned and waved for her tiger friend to come with them. He ran to join his adopted family.

Epilogue

Katie sat on the porch of her father's cabin and thought about how her ship, *Vixen*, looked out of place sitting in the clearing by the log structure. Although she had visited Nebula One several times in the last few years since her father moved here, she still thought her ship looked out of place.

Her father came outside carrying a portable communications unit and sat beside his youngest daughter. He spoke as he activated the unit. "Ben's on the com. You want to talk to him?"

She greeted her brother as she leaned in so she could see him.

She noticed the background had nothing but water, and she asked, "Ben, where are you guys at?"

Before Ben could answer her, Dylan leaned in and said, "Hi, guys. This place is so cool."

Ben nudged his friend out of the way so he could finish talking to his sister. Dylan yelled from the background, "Tyton says hi, too!"

Ben laughed and continued to answer Katie's question, "We are on a water world we named Aqua. It is so cool. The aquatic plants here produce enough oxygen to allow humans to survive here. We are preparing to go underwater exploring."

He pointed the camera at the small submarine. Dylan saw that the camera was on them. He patted Tyton, and they waved playfully. Ben turned back to himself.

"Falcon Intergalactic gave us the money for this cool stuff."

Katie felt a bit sad hearing that name. Ben spoke once more after a brief pause, "Well, Dad and Katie, I got to go. We do not have much daylight left. Talk to you guys soon." Katie and her father said a quick good-bye.

Before he signed off, Ben spoke quickly, "Oh, by the way, Bethany said to tell you all hello. She is real busy running Uncle Willie's company."

Ben signed off.

Katie stood and leaned against a post, and her father put his arm around her shoulder as he joined her.

Katie looked up just as her sister, Jennifer, and her tiger companion, Max, came over the hill. Mech 1 followed close behind. Shorty whistled a greeting to them, and Jennifer waved.

Katie smiled, as she thought of how her life was good despite the events of the recent past.

Cast of Characters

Katie: Commander of *Big Rock* station. After getting a master's degree in astronomy, she obtained a grant and built the station.

Jennifer: Captain of *Tiger's Pride*. She had originally studied to become a biologist; however could not keep from becoming attached to the animals under her care. She got a job with Falcon Intergalactic as a contract agent. She purchased *Tiger's Pride* at one of the company's surplus auctions.

Max: A Bengal tiger with a prototype cybernetic device designed to allow communication between humans and animals. Jennifer adopted him when his mother was killed during the terrorist attack in which Jennifer's mother was the target, while she was visiting her at school. He was named after the biologist who had helped save his life when Jennifer removed him and his siblings from his mother's womb. He was the only one to survive.

Ben: A biologist/cybernetic engineer who specialized in alien biological sciences. He invented Max's cybernetic device. He is under contract with Interstellar Alliance until he pays off his education loans, which he had applied for because he did not want to trouble his father.

Dylan: Ex-marine in the Interstellar Alliance military. He served the last two years in Interstellar Alliance military intelligence after being injured during combat late in the Mars War.

Tyton: Interstellar Alliance robotic marine unit. Dylan modified him after his series was taken out of service by the military. Programmed for ship maintenance, serves as ships copilot, and specializes in several types of combat. Note: Ben, Dylan, and Tyton travel aboard the *Saber II* in search of adventure. Tyton also became Dylan's constant companion after carrying him out of combat after his injury.

Boots: A cyborg/translator officer. He serves as the *Big Rock Science Station*'s second in command and as the station's translator officer. He is nicknamed Boots because he likes to wear twentieth-century cowboy boots. He joined the cyborg corps after the loss of his hearing and lower half of his right arm in a space battle near Jupiter. He served as an Interstellar Starfleet officer for eight years.

TU-413: A robotic technical unit assigned to the *Big Rock Science Station*. He is Boots' aide in charge of the station's robotic units and a standard bipedal robot. He uses a mobility pod most times. Note: Bipedal units use mobility pods to perform different tasks. The pods can hover, roll, and operate in space and are used to carry tools and other items needed by the robot units to perform tasks. In addition, they are beneficial in supporting the robot's weaker lower half.

Mech 1: The highest-ranking robot in the crew aboard *Tiger's Pride*. Mech 1 is short for Mechanical Unit No. 1. He and Max became friends. Being a robot, he does not show emotions, such as nervousness, in Max's company, and that is what draws Max to him. He became Jennifer's companion after the terrorist attack on Phobos.

Bethany: Jennifer's best friend, who is an agent in the Saturn Security Forces. She also is a new member of the elite combat unit known as Panthers, and her code name is Delta.

Panther: One of the founding members of the elite combat unit known as Panthers. He adopted the name when the unit disbanded during the Mars War due to split loyalties. He is currently employed by Falcon Intergalactic as a covert operative.

Shorty: A small computer specialist robot, commonly called a hacker unit. He became Katie's companion after developing a programming glitch called the puppy dog glitch, which caused him to become attached to her. He is always by her side.

Interstellar Alliance: Formerly known as Earth Interstellar Alliance. The organization was set up by the United Nations to govern Earth's colonies in outer space. It became independent from Earth after the Mars War. The organization maintains a Starfleet for protection and a small research fleet for space exploration. Katie's *Big Rock* science station was funded through a research fleet grant and falls under its command.

Falcon Intergalactic Freight Company: The largest freight company in the interstellar regions (beyond Earth's solar system). Its parent company is Falcon Intergalactic. In an attempt to cut costs after the Mars War, the Interstellar Alliance contracted the company for supply runs to its deep space colonies. William Hughes and his friend Benny Graham are the owners.

Interstellar Alliance Commando: First encountered at the battle at Uranus. It was developed in secrecy when alliance officials considered human and cyborg soldiers to be difficult to control.

Sasquatch orphans, Buford and Sasha: Inhabitants of Nebula One. They are members of the species known as Sasquatch. They are the youngest male and female of a family unit. The leaders of Nebula One allowed them to join Katie, Ben, and Jennifer after their family was killed when the Interstellar Alliance sent a robotic fleet to capture the world. They use a translation mask to communicate with humans. They took human names when they adopted Katie, Ben, and Jennifer as family.

Breanna: Ben, Jennifer, and Katie's cousin. Goes by the call sign of Bre, which is her nickname as well. She escaped the planet Mars to join the rebellion, just before the Chancellor of the Interstellar Alliance declared martial law on the planet. She assumed command of the warship *Sarah Elizabeth* while her captain, Bethany, was on Earth. She later became a fighter/bomber pilot with the Fighting Angel squadron.

The Fighting Angels Squadron: A group of female fighter pilots who came to join the rebellion from Earth. Their names were Anna Jo, Kiesha Shayna, and Lauren. They had been friends and basketball teammates of Jennifer's in school before the war. They met Breanna while she was on Earth and decided to come to Jennifer and her sibling's aide after she told them what was happening in the rebellion.

Hawk/Dalton: A childhood friend of Jennifer's, who became a mercenary along with his robot friend Warrior after the death of his parents. He was mentored by the mercenary called Scorpion. They took a job from the Alliance to do a recon mission on Nebula One, which he later found out was a mission to disable the planet's defenses. He joined the rebellion after he turned on his partner, when he wanted to go after Katie and Jennifer to collect the bounty on them.

Valkyrie: Jennifer's friend Jessica, who went by the call sign to protect her identity. She did this because her father was imprisoned on Mars and would be killed if Alliance officials knew she was part of the rebellion. She joined the Fighting Angel Squadron when they arrived.

Jared: A rebel pilot, who goes by the call sign Momma's Boy. He defected along with his squadron during the rebellion. He is a cousin to Katie, Jennifer, and Ben. Although Dylan and he are brothers, they have different mothers, so Dylan isn't related to the Graham siblings.

A. J.: The rebellion's agent on Mars. He and Katie were romantically involved in school.

Prime Minister Logan: The leader of Mars, who after learning of the corruption in the Alliance gathers allies and joins the rebellion. He brings with him twelve warships.

Rhino and Guardian: Robotic marine units who were part of the combat group at the factory near Uranus. They were assigned as bodyguards for the Sasquatch orphans, who reluctantly accepted them.

Warrior: Hawk's robotic partner since he was young. He is an old warrior-class robotic marine unit.

Ceres City: A once-thriving spaceport and mining colony built on the dwarf planet Ceres. It was abandoned by the mining company, which owned it because of constant pirate attacks during the Mars War. It is mostly home to pirates and criminals.

Ship Classifcations

Big Rock: Interstellar Alliance's research fleet science station, built on the surface of an enormous asteroid. It is equipped with ion propulsion-drive engines. It is capable of sublight and light speed travel. It is armed only for defense. It is a refurbished mining station that Katie acquired from her father's mining company, after the Interstellar Alliance approved her application for a research grant. It is presently stationed in the Orion Nebula sector.

Tiger's Pride: A refurbished Mars class Interstellar Alliance battle cruiser, with no affiliation with any organization. It is capable of sublight and light speed travel and is armed for defense and offense. Its skeleton crew is provided presently by Falcon Intergalactic Freight Company and is contracted to escort freighters on deep space supply runs to subsidize cost of maintaining the ship.

Saber II: A medium-sized Interstellar Alliance marine transport. It is moderately armed and has sublight and light speed engines. Purchased and modified by Ben, Dylan, and Tyton prior to Dylan's release from the marines.

Vixen: Its design is based on a twentieth-century Apache helicopter. It has been redesigned and modified for space and planetary flight. Its propellers are used for low atmosphere flight and retracted while in space flight. Slightly larger than the original craft, it is equipped with ion drive engines for sublight and light speed. Its weaponry and agility make it an impressive craft suitable for space missions. It is Katie's personal ship, which was a gift from her father on her twenty-first birthday. Katie named the ship this because a vixen is a mischievous girl or woman. That is exactly what she had been growing up into. Its rotor system is a special modification designed by her father.

Kit-Cat: A Saturn Security Forces S-17 Raider, which Bethany purchased at a surplus auction and uses as her personal ship.

Big Willie: A large space barge. It is used to transport space stations and other large structures through space for deployment and repair. It has a secret deck housing two squads of fighters (twenty-four). Privately owned but has close affiliation with Falcon Intergalactic Freight Company.

Little Maggie: A small-tracked vehicle that belonged to Ben, Jennifer, and Katie's mother. Katie kept it after the death of her mother. She fixed it up and fitted it with a laser turret. She named it in memory of her mother who had been killed years earlier in a terrorist attack on Mars by a group known as ARES.

Pinto: Boots' private ship. It is an earlier version of Katie's ship, *Vixen*. It has a single deck. It does not have a rotor system. It is named after the breed of horse. Boots had one as a youngster back on Earth.

X-13: A Special Forces corvette/prototype designed by the members of the combat unit known as Panthers. Only two were built, a single seat and a two-seat version. It never went into production because the unit was disbanded during the Mars War.

Lady Tiger: An old Mars marine attack corvette. While cleaning up the ship, Jennifer found it in one the numerous storage bays in *Tiger's Pride* hangar. She fixed it up and now uses it as her personal ship.

Lone Star: A Saturn-class destroyer, which is commanded by Boots at the battle near the outer rim of the solar system.

Sarah Elizabeth: A Saturn-class battle cruiser commanded by Bethany at the battle near the outer rim of the solar system.

Galaxy 12 and 14 fighters: A small one-man fighter. The Galaxy 12 was used during the Mars War, and the Galaxy 14 is an updated version. Panther and his rebel pilots use both fighters. Dylan's brother, Jared, pilots the Galaxy 14 model.

Interstellar Alliance's Robotic Cruiser: Developed early in the Rebellion by the Interstellar Alliance.

MS-1023: A mining station similar to *Big Rock*, although it does not have the capability to travel through space on its own. It depends on the barge *Big Willie* to move it from place to place. It is used by the rebellion as a command center.

Stinger: An old armor transport, which was owned by the mercenary Scorpion. Hawk took possession of the craft after his partner's death on Nebula One.

Cub: Hawk's personal ship. A small fighter transport, which is carried by the larger *Stinger* in the ship's armored vehicle clamps. After Hawk joined Scorpion, the craft was used mostly as an escort fighter on jobs the group took.

Star Cluster Fighter: Earth's main fighter. It is flown by the four pilots from Earth in the Fighting Angel squadron.

Jupiter Storm Fighter Bomber: A fighter bomber built by Jupiter's defense force. Jennifer has one as her personal fighter, and Breanna chooses it as her fighter when she becomes a fighter pilot.